Violet's Odyssey

Violet's Odyssey
Robert E Moulton

All rights reserved
Copyright © 2024
by Robert E Moulton

No part of this publication may be reproduced, distributed, or transmitted in any form or by any means, including photocopying, recording, or other electronic or mechanical methods, without the prior written permission of the publisher, except in the case of brief quotations embodied in critical reviews and certain other noncommercial uses permitted by copyright law.

ISBN: 979-8-89569-123-6

Violet's Odyssey

Robert E Moulton

Contents

Chapter 1

The Mysterious Meeting

"So what's yours say?" she asked, laughing.

I cracked open the cookie. "Your dearest wish will come true," I read off, and couldn't help but giggle.

She laughed hard at that. "... in bed! Sure! Of course that's what it says!"

"No, no, don't... !" But that's all I got out before she tickled me, and grabbed for the fortune.

She goggled. "I'll be damned – that's really what it says!"

I just gave her a hurt look, which sent her off into gales of laughter.

Not much later than that, we went to bed – and it was every bit as good as I'd been anticipating. There ... were some surprising aspects. And the next morning, now.... But I'm getting ahead of myself.

* * *

I'd met Ashley just earlier that day. It's silly, looking back at it later. I should have known.

Well. You always say you should have known, right? But of course life just does the utterly unexpected when you least expect it.

There's no way I could have known.

I was working my latest dead-end job; I'd just never seemed to engage with the whole idea of earning my keep, and it always showed. I just couldn't deal with managers, somehow.

So anyway, there I was, slinging coffee at the local café house in Paris. Or actually, in this case, mopping. Or actually, not mopping, much; rather, contemplating the wonders of the universe on a lovely spring day – i.e. staring out the window at the sunshine, waiting until I could get back to my reading and piddling around on the computer. Oh, I should probably mention that the Paris in question is in Tennessee, not France. It's a quiet little college town, good coffee houses, decent public library, all in all a nice place to live and contemplate the wonders of the universe.

A sudden deluge of frigid cold on my back jolted me back to present reality. I could say that this was the turning point of my life – and I would be entirely correct – but at the time, it just felt cold and wet. Foreshadowing is just a literary device, no matter what Ashley... Oh, wait, no, that's getting ahead again.

Anyway, the scene is still playing out, so let's get back to it.

"Oh, my! I'm so sorry!" Her voice was like music, and I turned around to behold quite possibly the most lovely woman I had ever seen, one hand covering her mouth and the other holding up a napkin, presumably to smear the bucket of lemonade she'd just spilled down my back. It certainly wouldn't be enough to soak it all up.

With my characteristic aplomb, I just stared down at her, speechless. Her skin was golden, her hair was a slightly darker shade of gold, her eyes were blue, her face was a dream, and the rest of her so shapely it hurt to look at her. There was nothing I could say or do to make that moment more perfect; I just drank her in and waited for time to restart.

"I'm so sorry," she said again, dabbing at my back with the napkin. "We have to get you out of those wet clothes!"

And with that, somehow she was dragging me out of the coffeeshop, somehow having placated my manager, and somehow we ended up at my apartment, where I was propelled bodily into the bathroom to change.

So I did. I checked the mirror, just to be sure I was still me. Yup. Gangly, mouse-colored hair, nondescript face, still a trace of acne from a very unfortunate adolescence that had left scars – and I don't just mean the acne, either. In addition to managers, girls were another subset of humanity I just somehow couldn't deal with.

I know I sound pretty typically emo. Sorry. I've always had an active internal life. Thoughts are so very much my only friends that I tend to see the rest of the world as actors on a stage, just more thoughts to amuse me. It makes me pretty boring at parties – although I do enjoy watching.

Taking a deep breath, now drily clothed, I stepped back into the living room. And – wonder of wonders – she was still there, checking out the books on my shelf as though she cared.

Hearing me, she turned, and stuck out a hand. "Hi, I'm Ashley." I think I could actually hear the odd spelling. "You looked like you needed a rescue."

I blinked. "A rescue?"

She just smiled. "So, you're into logic, are you?"

"Um, yeah. I guess." Smooth line, that. I have a thing for formal logic – it's just so ... ruly. With logic, you know where you stand.

"Me, too." She smiled at me some more. I had no idea how to respond. After some more smiling, she nodded and said, "How are we going to spend this lovely day, then?"

That left me so nonplussed I simply had no response. At which point an amazing thing happened. Ashley laughed – not at me. She just ... laughed at the absurdity of the entire conversation. And I started to laugh, too.

Let me explain. I am ... well, I was the person for whom the phrase "painfully shy" had been conceived. In any given situation – and not just with managers or girls – I could sometimes plot out what might be the right thing to say, but the process of calculation invariably took long enough that the moment had passed. I simply had to look at other human beings, navigating the maze of human relationships with some inborn facility I lacked, and wonder: how do they do it?

But I laughed with Ashley. Just like that, spontaneously!

So I took her to my favorite hiking spot, and we took a long walk. I didn't talk; the laugh had been enough self-revelation for one day, and miraculously, she seemed to know that – and strangest of all, she didn't seem to mind.

And as the day went on, it was the oddest thing. I felt

as though, when I had a thought, she kind of understood what I was thinking. She would suddenly smile, or frown, or even blink.

Logically, of course, that was impossible – unless my axioms were wrong. But if you start questioning your axioms, where are you? Unhinged entirely? So I convinced myself that it couldn't possibly be so. Clearly, I was just projecting my busy internal life onto her, probably because I was so incredibly fascinated by her physical beauty.

Well. So the afternoon passed, and we ended up pretty hungry, so we got some Chinese carry-out for dinner. While eating it, I made a few attempts at conversation, all of which Ashley rewarded with possibly over-enthusiastic responses.

But it worked. As conditioning, it worked. I opened up more and more, and she laughed more and more, and at some point, she opened up her fortune cookie, which read - I kid you not - "The distinctive and crucial feature in the study of man is the concept of action."

This appeared to be the single funniest thing that Ashley had ever experienced, and I had to laugh along with her. Finally, she got the laughter under control just enough to gasp out, "...in bed! Hahahaha!"

We laughed some more, and then ... well, I told you that part. And then ... we went to bed. Me. In bed. With a woman.

I'll be honest – I had no idea what to do. I mean, obviously I knew what to do – I just had no idea how to start without looking like an idiot. So as a default, I essentially laid there terrified. I didn't even have an erection.

Ashley smiled and gave a little chuckle. "Don't worry. I got this." Moving slowly, she helped me out of my clothes, then she took hers off – my heart rate tripled – and my erection problem was gone. I gulped, and her eyes crinkled. She reached across me, her nipples brushing across my chest, and turned out the light, plunging us into Stygian darkness.

Then, invisible, she kissed me gently, first on the mouth, and then moving down to ... well. To my erection. And then she took it into her mouth, and my entire body twitched with the sudden need to, to ... I couldn't think. The feeling of her mouth overtook my entire being. It was warm, wet, enveloping – I felt as though all of me were inside her, a warm, misty feeling throughout me. The focus of my building orgasm spread as well, all around my body, out to my fingertips, and as her tongue tickled me and coaxed me, I felt a scream of tension erupt from my throat as I had my very first non-solo orgasm.

I was drenched in sweat, and ready to relax, but she was still on me, and the warm feeling was still in my belly, and incredibly, I was building to another climax. My reading had indicated that this wasn't really in the cards, but I wasn't prepared to argue – even if I had wanted to protest, I couldn't. I was in thrall to this woman, utterly. Her tongue and lips probed me and caressed me, until another series of moans and screams took control of me, and just as my second orgam blasted through my brain, it almost seemed that her tongue was inside my penis, or maybe inside my scrotum; the sensations were like nothing I'd ever experienced.

And then I screamed again in ecstasy, some unknowable tension again tearing its way out of my heart, out of my chest, and into the ether, and still she didn't let me stop. I was bound to her, and now her hands were roving around my body, pulling here, stroking there, and the sensation on my skin was electric.

The third orgasm built more slowly – a third orgasm? My mind was too fuzzy to comprehend it, but my body was in no doubt concerning what it wanted and what was going to happen. My every muscle clenched in pleasure, I spread my legs wider and wider, allowing Ashley into me; it even seemed I could feel her fingers, slick with some lubricant (I wondered briefly where she had gotten it), move inside me – but that was crazy, and besides, the sensation triggered my orgasm, and with a third scream ...

I fell asleep.

Chapter 2

A New Identity

I awoke to birdsong, utterly relaxed and content, perfectly willing to lie there, nude, under the down comforter, and breathe the fresh morning air and listen to the birds, forever. I rubbed my face, wondering how long I'd slept. I felt relaxed to ... to an incredible extent, actually.

Until I realized, that is, that my bedroom didn't have a window, and I didn't own a down comforter.

"Morning, Sleepyhead!"

"Morning yourself, lover!" I chirped. My throat felt very odd, and I cleared it, or tried to.

Ashley chuckled. "It's not going to work."

"What won't?"

"Clearing your throat. Your voice has changed."

I sat up, scratching my chest. "My voice has changed? What does that mean?"

She gave me a very odd smile indeed. "It means, that

very shortly, you're going to be very, very surprised, and you might even hate me."

"See," I said, "That's the kind of cryptic remark that makes a man wonder about his woman."

She winced.

I frowned. "What? What's up, Ashley?" It was just dawning on me that I was having absolutely no trouble talking to her, but it didn't help – I still had no idea what was going on.

"Well," she finally said, "I had hoped you'd kind of figure part of it out on your own, but this scene is really not playing out as I'd thought. Just let me say two things, and then I'm going to go down and finish getting your breakfast ready. First, it's for the best, and second, no matter how much you might disagree with it being for the best, it's irreversible." And with that, she was gone, and I still didn't know what she was talking about, but breakfast sounded very, very good indeed

I got out of bed, just happening to notice that there was a full-length mirror on the wall, and ... Holy shit, I thought. No wonder my chest had felt so smooth, and my face, too, now that I thought about it.

The figure I saw in the mirror was clearly me – but it was also very unmistakably a girl. My shoulders were narrower, my feet and hands smaller, my face was pretty, and, well, my junk was gone. I mean, not amputated or anything, just ... no longer there.

I swallowed and closed my eyes, then shook my head.

I opened my eyes again and it was still the same. Skinny, flat-chested, knobby-kneed, looking maybe fourteen, and pretty. Really pretty, in that fresh-faced way that young girls have who are clearly going to turn into real knockouts in a few years.

Slowly, ever so slowly, I smiled. The girl in the mirror had never even heard of acne. I smiled more broadly. My teeth were perfect. My eyes were perfect. My cheekbones were perfect. My collarbones were perfect. I turned a flank, and yes, my ass was bony, but definitely showed significant promise of utter and thorough perfection.

I couldn't believe it.

So I did the obvious thing. I opened the door the mirror was mounted on, which unsurprisingly proved to be a closet, with a nice fuzzy bathrobe on a hook set uncomfortably high on the inside of the door. I stood up on tiptoe to reach it down, put it on, and padded barefoot down to the kitchen. It was a bit of a walk - the house was huge, and all of it very nicely decorated and furnished. The kitchen itself was colossal, with yards of granite countertop and a very nice stove indeed, featuring a very familiar cook.

"So," I said to Ashley's tense back, my voice still absurdly high-pitched. "What's for breakfast?" This was coy; a corpse could have smelled the bacon. My stomach growled – I was hungry.

She turned and looked me in the eye, for the first time without a trace of smile. "Bacon and eggs." Her eyelid twitched.

I sat down at the counter and looked at my nails. "It smells great. I'm ravenous."

Without a word, she dished out a huge plate of food for me and sat down across from me. I dug in.

I swallowed a big bite, and said "So."

Ashley perked up. "So!"

"So I'm a soprano now." Very odd, that my voice no longer resonated in my chest.

She swallowed.

I smiled at her. "Thanks."

"Oh, God," she said, "I'm so sorry, this was the first ... what?"

"You heard me. Thank you." I stuffed more bacon into my mouth.

"You - you don't mind?"

I tilted my head to the side, still chewing. "Do you believe in fate?"

She blinked. "Well, yes, actually."

"Remember my fortune?"

"Your dearest... What - your dearest wish was to be a girl?"

I took another bite, then snorted. "You make it sound really weird."

"No, no," she protested. "I'm, I guess I'm just relieved."

"Don't worry about it." I shrugged. "It is weird."

"But ..." She stopped for a moment. "But you're not gay."

I shook my head. "What does that have to do with it?"

She opened her mouth, then closed it. As the gigantic plate of bacon and eggs was inexplicably empty now, I took the opportunity to serve myself some orange juice and pour milk on some cereal. I was still hungry. Presently, she started talking again.

"So, um, here I am with a whole bunch of things to tell

you," she said, "but I'm just too flabbergasted to get my thoughts in order. I've never done this before."

I raised my eyebrows. "Neither have I."

She laughed at that. "God help me, you are just adorable." She sighed. "OK, I owe you some explanations, so I'll start. First, and I know this sounds crazy, but -"

"Magic works," I said quickly, then took another bite of cereal.

She looked proud, and ... ambitious, somehow. "Right. Right. Magic obviously works, because here you are, you're still you, but you're eight inches shorter and you're a girl without any surgery or anything."

"Wait, what? I'm shorter? Stand up for a minute."

She did, and I did. Yesterday, she'd come up to my chin. Today, either she'd grown or she was right and I'd un-grown, because I was looking slightly up at her eyes.

"Wow," I said. "I'm petite." I reached down another box of cereal, with a little difficulty. The cabinets had been mounted very high on the wall for some reason. Oh, wait, I thought. It's not you, cabinets. It's me.

"That's why you're hungry," Ashley went on. "The, um, the transition takes a lot of energy, and you're growing back out of your childhood, too. You're what, 28?"

"Twenty-six," I said. "I'm going to be getting old?"

Her mouth curled up. "Oh, you'll get old, all right — over time. You just won't look it. How old do you think I am?"

"Hard to say. You act like an adult, but put you in a cheerleader's dress and I'd guess about 19."

She nodded. "And that's just about how you'll look in a few weeks."

"So, how old are you really?"

"My name is Connor MacLeod of the clan MacLeod. I was born in 1518 in the village of Glenfinnan on the shores of Loch Shield, and I canna die."

"That's the worst attempt at a Scottish accent I've ever heard, and it's not an answer."

She grinned. "Well, it's a lie anyway. I can die – maybe – but it's damn hard to achieve. And I was actually born right here in America."

I waited. "When?"

She shrugged. "We hadn't invented calendars yet."

"That's absurd. You're clearly not Native American."

"Oh?" Suddenly she was, without any particular transition – darker skin, long, straight, glossy black hair, slight epicanthic folds on black eyes. Then, in a slow fade, she returned to her California Cheerleader look. "I look like any woman, but my default appearance, how I look when I'm not thinking about it, changes slowly over time to match the people I see on a daily basis. As will yours. It's a sort of protective coloration – stand out too much, or even stay the same person too long, and they will do their damndest to kill you, especially if you're a woman." She looked at her fingernails. "That's been the worst of it. Like you, I was born a man."

A light dawned. "Ah. And unlike me..."

"Yeah. Unlike you, I was not too happy about the change. I tried to kill myself. Almost worked, too."

"You look pretty healthy."

She smiled ruefully. "Yes. Yes, I do."

"So how did you do it?"

"Oh, different ways. Stabbing didn't work no matter

where I stabbed myself. Drowning didn't work. Jumping from a tall tree onto jagged rocks hurt, a little – but didn't work. Finally, I came upon the idea of building a really big fire and immolating myself."

"But it didn't work." I was appalled.

She gestured at herself. "Nope. All it did was knock me out for a while."

"A while?"

"When I woke up, you Europeans were here."

"And that was?"

"About three hundred fifty years ago."

I had nothing to say to that. Amazingly, though, I finally felt full. I put a hand into my bathrobe onto my stomach, which was palbably swollen. My skin was so smooth, and for just a moment my hand strayed downwards to my hairless crotch. I had never felt less sexual, which was odd, as I had always had sexual fantasies about being female.

Ashley was watching. "You won't feel much for a couple of weeks."

I could feel myself blushing. "Wh- what do you mean?"

She grinned, not really at all mocking. "You're physically a child again right at the moment. You won't really have physical feelings of sexuality until you go through puberty again. Which, lucky you, is starting today on an accelerated schedule – but your clock has been reset."

I nodded. "I guess that makes sense. So ... will I be a lesbian, or what?"

She shrugged. "Luck of the draw, babe. I'm personally hoping you'll still like girls, but there's no telling."

"Huh. Well, given present company, I think I agree. It would be a shame after last night if we couldn't do that again."

"That wasn't last night, hon. That was five days ago. You've been asleep for a while."

My heart skipped a beat. "What? But my job!"

That made her laugh out loud. "Your job? Looking like that? You've heard of child labor laws, right?"

"But how will I live?"

"This is my house. I own it outright, and have for fifty years, and it's not the only house I've got. Living a long time is a great advantage when it comes to wealth accumulation, and you are the closest thing to offspring I can have. You can have anything here you want."

"But ..."

"No buts. I've had your things packed up from your apartment and brought here. The clothes won't fit, but I know you'll want your books and your PlayStation."

I stopped, mouth open. Actually, she was right. The books were really all I cared about at all from my previous life. Everything else was disposable. I didn't even have friends or family to speak of; my aunt had raised me and I'd escaped her as soon as it was practical to do so, and as I've explained, friendship wasn't my strong suit. I talked to some people online, but I could still do that.

"OK," I said. "I'll stay here for a while. Then we'll see."

She looked really happy for the first time this morning.

Suddenly, I yawned enormously. "Goodness! I should be well-enough rested after five days, but I could use a nap."

"You'll spend a lot of time sleeping over the next

couple of days. And eating. It's like being a teenager again, except compressed in time." She was smiling somewhat indulgently, but I didn't get the sense she was laughing at me at all. Actually, I felt very secure knowing she was watching out for me. But the table looked very soft, and I put my head on my arms, and that was all she wrote.

Chapter 3

What is a Magic User

WHEN I WOKE UP, IT WAS DARK AND VERY QUIET, AND I was in my bed again, the bathrobe back on its hook in the open closet door. Ashley was sleeping in a large armchair to the side of my bed, and my heart felt very warm and weepy to see her. I puffed up my pillow and turned on my side, looking at her, and drifted off thinking about how lucky I was to have this new life, and wondering what it was going to be like, not only being a woman but having a real ... family, I guess, and true friend, for the first time in my life.

I had some odd dreams about being at work at some of my old jobs, except being a girl, and usually naked. And then there was the one where I was Hermione Granger. That's the one that woke me up with a gasp. It was daylight again.

I vaguely recalled something about ... no, it was gone. But the tingling and warmth in my belly weren't, and even more strangely, my nipples were standing up. I massaged them, which felt good, and noticed that the skin around them had grown a little puffy.

"That was fast," I said aloud. I felt my groin. It was a little moist, and I could feel a little silky hair there. Hadn't Ashley said it would take a few weeks to hit my new puberty? It certainly seemed that it was here already. It was definitely a nice feeling to stroke my ... (I had to gulp) my clitoris.

With a little effort, I pulled my hand away and sat up in the bed, my legs over the side. I thought maybe they reached a little further down to the floor today.

Standing up on legs that suddenly seemed wobbly, I staggered to the closet door and closed it to look in the mirror, and gasped for the second time. I looked distinctly older this morning, maybe seventeen and definitely closer to being a woman. My hips looked like hips, for one thing, and while still skinny, it was possible to see that I was going to have some serious curves any day now. My face, if possible, was even prettier, and I bit my lip. God. I was getting horny looking at myself in the mirror.

But I smelled food, and my ravenous hunger was back, so I grabbed the bathrobe and pelted back down the stairs.

It occurred to me that I hadn't actually gone to a bathroom or bathed in a very long time now. But as I didn't feel the need to pee, I figured Ashley must have that covered. Somehow.

Sure enough, there she was, frying more eggs and bacon. Protein was clearly indicated, and I came up behind her and hugged her from the back, kissing her neck.

"Yikes! I didn't hear you!" She turned and gave me a

hug. It felt good, and I still felt loose and warm inside. Maybe I did still like girls. I hoped so.

"Hey," I said. "You're not any shorter. I thought I was supposed to be a growing girl!" I squirmed a little; the terry cloth of my robe felt strange on my nipples all of a sudden.

She pulled the front of the robe aside for a moment. "Hmm," she said, letting go before I could even react. "You do seem to be growing. That's actually very interesting. Not at all how it went for me." She pulled at her lip, which I found rather attractive.

"But here's the thing with magic," she went on. "There are literally as many ways to power as there are magic users. So your development will be uniquely yours."

I blinked. "Wait. You mean I'm going to be a ... a magic user?"

She laughed. "Well, yeah! What did you think, I just took some random guy off the street and turned him into a little girl for my own inscrutable and probably immoral purposes?"

"Uh, let's just say I hadn't thought about it at all yet. I've known you for less than a day of waking time. But yeah, when you put it that way, I guess... I guess I figured that sounded pretty good to me."

"You may be the strangest person I've ever met," she said, shaking her head. But she was still smiling. "Which bodes well! Strange is great, in magical terms. The stranger the ways in which you can apprehend the universe, the more effective you will be.

"Magic, you see," she continued, "is a question of seeing things in a different way and making the world agree with you. Or rather, it's a matter of reorganizing things." She pulled her lip again. It was rather endearing. "Well. Magic is hard to verbalize, as you'll no doubt find out at your own speed."

"So what happens now? Wax on, wax off? Catching flies with chopsticks? Training montage?"

"Pfft. One magic user can't train another. Everybody's system of magic is entirely sui generis. Once I've started you on the path, all I can do is talk to you about it, show you some books that hopefully won't hinder your comprehension as much as they help it, and introduce you to some possibilities. And be your friend."

"With benefits?" I asked. I swear, it slipped out without my thinking about it.

"I'm not going to say no," she shrugged. "But just– Wait. Are you serious?"

I swallowed. "Well. I had some really strange dreams, and I kind of woke up ... um, in the mood, if you know what I mean."

She goggled. "I certainly doknow what you mean, but this is really unusual!" She flipped a mass of eggs and bacon onto a plate. "But I also know that you need to eat before we even think about any other biological processes, so eat up."

"You make a good argument," I said, and sat at the table and got to work.

She stood there, leaning back against the counter and pulling her lip some more.

"While you eat, let me get some basic explanations out of the way. If you're already advanced in puberty after two days, you're moving a lot faster than anybody I've heard of, and here's the thing. A lot of magic is bound up with sex.

Hence the gender flip – it makes sense in context, really. But if you're already feeling sexual feelings, you're going to have to know some stuff now, and after breakfast you'll probably fall asleep again for a day or two.

"Next time you wake up, there's no telling what you'll have to deal with, so you eat and I'll talk.

"Here's the thing. Magic is inherently based on your worldview, and nothing affects the human worldview quite so much as sex. A lot of the myths about witches and magic users have some basis in fact, of course, and one of the biggies is that virgins are better at magic."

I wrinkled my brow. "But I'm not a virgin any more. We had sex all night the first day we met."

"Ah!" she cried, putting up a finger. "You'd think that! But here's the first weirdness you need to know. Only sex in your birth gender makes a difference. As a man, you're still a virgin."

"Oh," I said. "A lot of my memories of that night make more sense now."

She laughed. "Haha, yeah, I suppose that must have been confusing."

"I was kind of beyond confusion." I stretched, and said in a lower voice, "Parts of me aren't very confused right at the moment, though."

"Incredible!" She looked very excited, in a disappointingly nonsexual way. "You are just astounding!" She waved her hands, then started counting on her fingers. "Anyway, here's the thing, in as brief a list as possible. First, virgins are stronger. Second, outward women are stronger. Third, people who have sex can be stronger. Yeah, that's a nice little double-bind there. Fourth, introverts are stronger.

Remember how I said the stranger the worldview, the better? An extrovert tends to go with the crowd; they make great minions. A vibrant inner life makes the sorcerer. Fifth..." She thought a moment, looking adorable. "I can't think of a fifth right now."

I was full already. And honestly, I had to interpret the feelings in my belly and chest right now as being so horny I could hardly stand it. I had a strong urge to jump on her and ... and ... now there were definitely parts of me that were confused. I couldn't very well penetrate her with a penis any more.

"Ashley?" I managed, in a somewhat strangled way.

"Yes, dear?" She was still thinking about her next point.

"I have to tell you that I'm definitely certain I still like girls."

She blinked. "You look pretty tense, babe. Are you saying...?"

I nodded, not really able to say anything coherent.

"I remember some pretty powerful feelings in my second puberty," she said, "and you seem to be getting it all a lot faster."

"Ashley!" I ground out. "Less talk, more sex. I'm not sure how to go about it, but I want t-to fuck you."

She jumped over to me, and took my hand to lead me back up to the bedroom. "Oh, yes, that's the tension that will drive your little powerhouse later. You'll learn to manage it, but right now, there are some things we can do to make you feel better."

We got to the bedroom, and I gulped, pretty sure I knew what she meant. So I wasn't too surprised to turn around to sit on the bed and to find her very close to me, indeed. Gently, she undid the bathrobe that had been my sole clothing for the past ... however long it had been, and slid it off my shoulders. I shivered at the touch of her hands – my skin seemed far more sensitive than I thought possible.

She smiled. "Women's skin is more sensitive, isn't it? That's one thing that makes this so much more worthwhile." Her hands were firm as they turned me around and started massaging my back, moving up and down and releasing tension I hadn't even started to detect yet.

"Yeah," she said. "This is a lot, all of a sudden. And then to go through puberty on fast-forward in a different gender on top of that is going to be stressful even if youare asleep through a lot of it." She flipped me over and my heart skipped a beat.

"You poor thing, you look like a deer in the headlights." She bent over and kissed me, and a wave of heat ran through my entire body.

"Well, look at this," she said suddenly, kissing the puffy area around my nipple. It ... squished, oddly. Not in a bad way, though.

I looked down at it, and Ashley felt it gently. "Your tits have grown since you got up."

Amazed, I sat up and cupped one breast. There wasn't much, but there was enough to cup. I looked up at Ashley, a little panicky, and she just pushed me back and kissed me some more. I could feel my nipples standing up as she kissed and licked them – they were so sensitive! The electric feeling kept shooting out until suddenly, quite unexpectedly, with a little soprano whine, I orgasmed and she giggled.

Then she got down to business at my crotch. I was already more than ready, and eagerly spread my legs, pushing up into her fingers as I built towards another orgasm. All too soon, it came, explosively, and I moaned in ecstasy as I relaxed and realized that I was falling asleep again.

I had wet dream after wet dream as I slept. I had long since trained myself to wake up at the climax of a wet dream to clutch myself until I could get a Kleenex down to catch the semen. I detest wet pajamas and sheets. Now, though, there was nothing to clutch, and I quickly stopped waking up at all, only rousing partially for a blurry look around, sometimes day, sometimes night. I seemed to sleep about two days before finally coming to full consciousness again, sometime just after dawn, from the light and the birdsong.

I wasn't alone in bed, either. Ashley (I presumed) was spooned behind me, sound asleep with one trim arm flung protectively over me and clutching me beneath what were unmistakeably now my breasts. I looked at them in amazement; from this angle, they looked really good.

My hair had grown out while I slept, but I didn't want to move, for fear I'd wake Ashley. I gingerly reached an arm up to brush the worst of it out of my eyes, and pulled some out to look at it more closely. It wasn't really mousy brown any more, except at the tips; it was shot through with reddish gold strands. My skin color had changed, too, to a lovely tanned shade, as though I'd recently spent a week or two at Cozumel and not sound asleep in bed dreaming of sex. Curiouser and curiouser.

Chapter 4

Breakfast and Secrets

Ashley suddenly heaved a great sigh and squeezed me tighter as she woke up, and I was acutely conscious of the fact that she was also naked, her breasts deliciously compacted against my back.

"Are you awake?" she murmured, and I nodded, then twisted around in her arms for a kiss. Our breasts intermeshed in wondrous multiplicity, and my nipples essentially went spang against her.

"Yes," I said. "I had the most interesting dreams."

She snorted a little laugh. "I know, dear. I could feel them. I think the mundanes nearby must have felt them, or at least I can't see how they could avoid it."

I gasped. "What? Seriously?"

She nodded ruefully. "Yep, as a magic user, you ... project. One of the reasons we make so few new magic users, to be honest. Fortunately, we're well out in the country here and there are almost no mundanes about to start with."

"Oh, how embarrassing." I could feel the blush down to my chest.

"Not at all, dear. Just a fact of life. I can tell you though, the past two days have been exciting. Literally." She smiled and stretched, and on impulse, I ducked beneath the covers to try out some of what she'd taught me about the female body over the past two nights ... or whenever they'd been.

She tasted sweet, and I lapped it up eagerly as she drew in her breath and said something like, "Oh my! This is acceptable compensation!" But that was about all she managed before I got her into the same moaning state I'd already experienced. I experimented a little with slowing down and speeding up, and enjoyed for the first time the feeling of being the one in control. It made me wet, and I tried fingering myself, with quite pleasant results. My rhythm faltered as I neared climax, but it only seemed to make her more frenzied, and soon, she mashed my head down into herself and, keening her joy, obviously orgasmed, maybe twice. So did I.

"You're such a fast learner," she sighed. "Oh, did I ever need that."

"So," I said brightly, "What's for breakfast?"

She laughed. "You've already eaten all my bacon and eggs, so I thought we could go out for something. Although I do have some cookies if you want one."

"I thought you just said we were well out in the country. I'm too hungry to drive into a town." I didn't think I could manage a cookie right away – I wanted a real breakfast.

"Just trust your Aunt Ashley," she said.

"I never woke up like that with my aunt," I mumbled, but she prudently didn't hear me, instead leaping out of bed.

"Well, get dressed, girl!" And with that she was gone.

Oops. I honestly hadn't thought of that – get dressed, girl? I sighed, and stood up, then nearly sat back down at the vision of loveliness in the mirror. Good God, it had been clear I would grow up to be a real looker, but this was ridiculous.

My hair was indeed subtly different, with reddish gold throughout. My face had somehow matured into something fundamentally better than the very pretty girl I'd seen before. My bone structure, already perfectly cut, somehow ... Well. I was all just "somehow" far, far prettier, and it took physical effort to tear my glance away.

I was gorgeous, and moving gracefully without thinking about it, although I'd always been a gawking, gangly kind of boy. There must be something... well, something magical about it. I went over to the door that I knew wasn't a closet, hoping it was a bathroom so I could wash off. It was, in fact, a bathroom, but I found I didn't really need to wash off. This was a little confusing, as I had clearly felt a great deal of sloppy moistness while fingering myself, but it was not only gone without a trace, but even my pubic hair (now that I had some again) was neat and orderly. I looked at my face in the mirror. Every hair was in place. Even my breath smelled sweet, although I hadn't brushed for at least a week now, and had gone to bed directly after eating, twice in a row. A quick sniff under my arm just smelled like healthy woman, with a touch of perfume.

"So I guess I'll just get dressed, then," I told my reflection.

"That's what I said!" said Ashley from outside the door – already perfectly dressed and made up, which I knew was impossible.

I stamped one bare foot in a way I suddenly perceived as utterly adorable, and said, "Ashley, this doesn't make sense at all! I look perfect! We just had sex, and I'm not a bit messy, I've been asleep for a week and I don't need to brush my teeth. I haven't even freaking gone to the bathroom yet, and don't need to. What is going on?"

She held up that finger again. "Lesson two! And in the meantime, put these on." She pointed at the bed, where she'd laid out a lacy camisole and panties, a short skirt, and a really cute blouse, and even flat shoes. I just stared for a minute. I had to admit I liked being a girl, but going out dressed like that? In front of other people? Insanity.

"What about my old clothes?" I asked, then hit my head.

"Ha. Your old clothes don't even fit. You were nearly six feet tall, and now you most definitely aren't six feet tall. And that's only the height, dear."

Grumbling, I pulled on the panties. "They do feel comfortable. What about lesson two, then?" I put on the camisole and she helped me get it laying right, and then helped me on with the skirt.

"Well. Here's the thing. You and I aren't actually women, you see. When you get down to it, we're really magical creatures, based loosely on succubi. Different people do this differently, but I naturally felt most comfortable making you into what I was made into back in the day."

I shrugged, clumsily buttoning up the blouse, with its wrong-way buttons. "That makes sense, I guess."

"So, yes. It may be weird, but it really doesn't take much getting used to – you will simply always be attractive. Your hair will be messed when you want it to look that way, and otherwise it will always be fresh from the hairdresser. Your breath will always be sweet, and salad will never stick to your teeth. You will never have a period. You don't need to wash, you don't need to shave, and you don't need to go to the bathroom. You do need to eat, of course – and you can enjoy it! Because the only time you'll ever gain weight is if society's standards of beauty change. Why, I went to Hawai'i once and gained fifty pounds in three days! Oh, what a lovely feast week that was." She got a little vague and misty-eyed.

I put on the shoes, then looked in the mirror. Sheesh. Now I was just prettier. It was like a curse.

I waved a hand in front of her eyes, and blinked when I noticed my nails were painted. I had certainly not painted them, and I was pretty sure they hadn't been painted when I got up. They matched the blouse.

She laughed at my surprise. "It's like a built-in glamor, really. Instead of being a woman, you're more like a symbol of femininity. It still counts as being a woman for magic use, without any of the downside except for, you know, being seen as a symbol of femininity. So, ready for breakfast?"

"And how! I'm not as ravenous as the past two times, but I could still kill a good breakfast."

"Hold my hand, then."

I did, and then we were ... elsewhere. She held the door for me, and we went into a cozy little diner, where they were just gearing up for breakfast. The early morning sun appeared to be lower, suddenly.

"A nice little place I know, about one time zone west. You didn't think I'd make you wait, did you, babe?"

I looked at her, and did a double-take. Instead of the cheerleader I knew, suddenly she was a very well-preserved motherly type, maybe just shy of 40 but clearly keeping very fit indeed.

The waitress came up to seat us.

"How many, ma'am? Just you and your daughter?"

"Yes, dear, thank you."

She navigated me over to a table, where I managed to sit down without collapsing. Suddenly, it was all just a little too much. She gave me a wry smile. "Sorry, I guess I'm having a bit of a joke at your expense here. Just ... relax and have a nice breakfast, OK?"

I nodded shakily. "OK. That sounds doable." I stared at the menu.

"You might not learn to teleport. You'll almost certainly be able to change your appearance, like I have; as I said, that's part of my nature, and now yours. But everybody's a new book." She looked down. "Oh, try their skillet breakfasts, they're really quite good."

I couldn't focus on the menu anyway, and nodded.

"Teleportation is how I found you, you know. Oh, surely you didn't think it was a chance encounter? You reeked of prototypical magic, even though you didn't know it. You were actually screwing the rest of us up."

I smiled. "I've read the Witches of Karres."

She gave me a blank look. "The what?"

"The Witches of Karres. You must not be much of a science fiction fan. It's a book about a space captain who rescues three little girls who turn out to be adepts in the use of klatha magic energy. When he takes them back to their home planet, he can't stay, because he messes up the focus of everybody on the planet."

She looked surprised. "Really! That's actually not too far off! You certainly were messing up half of this planet. I was sent to take care of you."

"What, by initiating me into the club?"

"No, by getting you laid to defuse you, actually." She grinned. "But when I actually met you, I couldn't resist. You made me laugh. I fell in love, and saw my opportunity, and here we are. You're the first new magic user in over a century, and some people are probably not going to be too happy with me."

I gulped. "Uh, how not too happy?"

She shrugged. "Well, we're all pretty eccentric and introverted to boot. We'll just cross those bridges when we come to it. As a bona fide magic user and not an almost-user, you're already far, far less disruptive. You're starting to channel things instead of just muddying up the water, so to speak. For a while, they'll think I just boffed you and been done with it, and most of them won't care, just as long as your wild magic was tamed."

Oh, great. I was going to be the sworn enemy of a bunch of alpha geeks entrusted with the keys to the world's root mode. I slumped down, just as the waitress came and introduced herself. She was cute. Weirdly, I was cuter, and very aware of it, but I still couldn't help but imagine how she might taste.

"I think we'll both have the breakfast skillet, won't that be good, dear?" She aimed the last at me, and I nodded. The waitress, seeming a little flustered, wrote it down and hurried off to the kitchen.

Ashley giggled. "You'd better turn the power down on your girlfriend there. I think she's ready to come home with you right now."

I gulped yet again. "What?"

"Remember how I said you project? It's not just when you're asleep." She was having an infuriatingly good time.

"Sorry, it's not like I have any experience with this, you know."

"Oh, I'm sorry, I know, dear. Just ... think unsexy thoughts if you can." She was still chuckling.

"You know," she said suddenly, "I'm going to need to start calling you a name. 'Babe' is good occasionally, but it gets monotonous, doesn't it?"

She'd never asked. "I'm actually D–".

She slapped a hand over my mouth. "No. No. Don't tell me, don't tell anybody, ever. Your true name is gone with your old self, and let's keep it that way. Bad enough you're still in the records, and we're going to have to fix that. But this is another way mythology gets it right. Names have power, a lot of power. I'm going to call you ... I'm going to call you Violet, because you blush so becomingly."

I blushed at that, presumably becomingly, and felt incredibly self-conscious. I looked around briefly at the other people in the diner. I couldn't help but notice that the awareness of every male in the place was directly on me, and many of the females as well. It was like I was a magnet. Ashley didn't even seem aware of it. Maybe, after 250 years, she was just used to being the center of attention at all times, but it was creeping me out. I slumped down in my chair some more, trying to look plain and – I was pretty sure – failing.

She was still explaining something about magic, something I was sure would be crucial to understand, especially once the rest of the club came down on both of us for my existence, but I couldn't concentrate on her words at all. I just felt the weight of everyone's studious non-attention, and tried not to think about how extremely fuckable I felt, and a pressure built up in my head. It pounded like a sinus headache. I could almost hear voices in it, maybe the voices of the people around me.

Suddenly, a clear silence rang out, if you'll pardon that turn of phrase. Like the bells of the Unseen University, measures of silence cutting through the din of Ankh-Morpork, except continuous. Abruptly, my feelings of sexual tension cut off as well – and so did Ashley's monologue, eyes bugging out of her head. For a moment, she even lost her age glamor and looked like a teenager again, but she rapidly regained her composure and looked discreetly around the room. Everywhere but directly at me, actually.

Conversation picked up, too, and I noticed that nobody at all was looking at me now.

The waitress came with our drinks. "Oh," she said, "Where's your daughter?"

I'm right here, I thought. Something kept me from speaking out loud; I felt like old times, tongue-tied.

Ashley smiled. "She just went to the bathroom, dear. Thank you for the coffee."

"Oh, no problem, ma'am," she said. She paused, as if wanting to say something else, but Ashley smiled at her in a vaguely dismissive way, and she fled.

"You are still here, aren't you?" said Ashley very quietly.

It took monumental effort to speak, but I managed to squeak, "Yes. I'm still sitting right here."

"Good Lord," she said. "You've been conscious as a magic user for all of a hour and a half and you're so inconspicuous even I can't feel you or your thoughts."

I couldn't say anything to that. I also couldn't seem to relax it at all. So I just sat there in silence, every bit as miserable as before my transformation, until the waitress came back with our food. She looked pretty perplexed at the fact that half my Coke was gone even though I still hadn't come back, and for a moment she looked as though she was going to say something, but something in Ashley's expression, and maybe something radiating from my little bubble, drove her off again.

The food smelled wonderful and my hunger came back abruptly, all at once. I tucked in immediately, and suddenly Ashley laughed.

"Hey, there you are. Still pretty indistinct, but food is good for the soul, isn't it?"

I laughed and nodded, and something in my heart loosened up. The waitress, behind the counter, looked over and did a double-take to see me in my seat, eating, and Ashley smothered a giggle.

"Jeez, I won't be able to come back here for a while after this kind of show." She grinned to show she didn't mean it.

"About all that name stuff you were just talking about", I said, "So, Ashley isn't actually your ..." I stopped, feeling stupid.

"No, Violet, Ashley is not a Native American name. You're the only person who calls me that, because I made it up just for you. Now it has a little bit of power over me, because you know me by it and I actually gave it to you, but that's a really small risk, and it's certainly one I'm willing to take. My true name, the one my mother called me and the one I chose in the company of my brothers when I became a man, is not only dead and forgotten, the language it was in is dead and forgotten, along with my people. Believe me," she shuddered, "Anonymity is a far better way to live. You don't want someone to get that power over you."

"Even you?"

"Especially me, Violet. I have enough power over you as it is – you are my creation and in a sense my daughter, and you will grow to be my sister, and I know you better right now than anybody else in the world – but over time our relationship will change. May it not change so much we become enemies, but ... I have lived a very long time indeed, and one thing these centuries have taught me is that things change, and people change, and good times cannot last."

For a moment, she didn't look 40, she looked 400, or

4000, infinitely ancient and melancholy. A tear rolled down my cheek.

"Only 250 years was enough to make you so sad?"

"Oh, my little blushing flower, I was not young when I nearly succeeded in dying. I lost count for many, many seasons, but I may have lived nearly a thousand years then. Certainly long enough to bury all my brothers, their descendants, and every nation who even resembled mine. Languages changed and evolved while I despaired, and still I could not die." She stroked my cheek. "How I treasure your innocence, my blossom."

The huge breakfast was feeling like lead in my stomach. I couldn't imagine how anybody could deliver prose like that and mean it, but man, she pulled it off.

I heaved a sigh, almost a sob, and changed the subject. "So what about your, uh, progenitor or whatever? Is she the same as us?"

Ashley smiled and sat back. "Ha, well, there's an interesting thing actually. Most magic users are made. I was not, not by any human. I was changed by the Trickster himself."

At this point I was ready to believe anything. "What, Coyote?"

"We didn't call him coyote, of course. He was a raccoon to us – I mean, really, a trickster without hands? Those people are crazy. Ours had hands, but he was the same god, I'm sure."

I boggled. "No, seriously? A god took you, as a man, and turned you into a, well, something like a woman? Just like that?"

She nodded, utterly matter-of-factly. I wondered if she

was crazy. I wondered if it even mattered. "Just like that. I was about fifty years old, I think."

"And still a virgin?"

She laughed. "Yes, actually. Shortly after I took my name but before I took a wife, I went out hunting buffalo, and got gored." She shrugged. "I lived, and made sure the buffalo did not – but I lost my manhood. The bull had castrated me. After that, I sort of became the people's medicine man. As a eunuch, I couldn't be a regular warrior or hunter, of course, but people respected my loss and saw a certain power in it. And we needed a new medicine man anyway; our old one had died.

"I was pretty good at it, too. I spoke to the gods on a regular basis – gods were thick on the ground in those days, but of course that's because we believed it to be so. Now, you don't, and the old gods are mostly gone or dormant. Believe me, it's better this way. gods are capricious.

"I had always gotten along well with Raccoon, the Trickster. He thought my castration was hilarious, and especially appreciated that I still kept the horns of the buffalo with me as a memory that I had killed my killer. And for a man, I learned a great deal of magic, both from the gods and from my own experimentation. Of course, as a man I could only go so far, although I didn't know that at the time.

"One night, Trickster was at my fireside with me, telling tales and drinking beer and laughing the sun up as only Trickster could do. We had great days back then, Trickster and I. And then I told him, 'Raccoon, I miss my manhood with all my heart and would have been the world's greatest warrior if I had not lost it. But what I would like even more is to understand the weaving of the world better.' That's what I called magic back then. It's actually a better name than 'magic', of course, because it describes it instead of just saying it's what mages do.

"Well, Trickster grinned, but he always did that. And then he chuckled, and that was nothing new, either. And then he outright laughed, and I laughed with him, because that's what we did all the time. 'My friend,' he said, 'I have thought of the perfect gift I can give you, and so I shall!' And then he laughed and laughed, and I stopped laughing, because it just then occurred to me that attracting too much attention from a god isn't always a good thing. And then I fell asleep.

"I slept for five days, they told me, as I regressed in age, and I woke up a little girl just as you did, although as I had been a eunuch before that, nobody noticed that part but me. And even though I regained my adulthood in another month or so, I still stayed a girl forever after." She finished the rest of her coffee, then said, "They sure did notice that, and I hated Trickster for many years, but he was right. It was the perfect gift. When I finally understood that, Trickster and his brothers were nothing but a memory to me, and a myth to everyone else. I do miss him."

I was speechless. After a while, though, I just had to ask. "Beer? You drank beer in prehistoric America?"

She snorted. "You don't miss much, do you? Don't you see? Trickster was Loki, too. He always brought the beer, straight from Valhalla." She smiled and shook her head. "Man, could that guy party."

"I think you may have destroyed my sanity entirely, Ashley. I think I actually believe you."

"Oh, don't worry. The world turns out to be not only stranger than you imagine, it's stranger than you can imagine. And the more you can imagine, the stranger it gets." She waved for the check. "Let's blow this popsicle stand."

The waitress smiled warmly at me and slipped me a piece of paper as we left. I looked at it. It was her phone number. Wordlessly, I showed it to Ashley, who just smirked and raised an eyebrow.

I blew out a breath. "To think I used to have troubles picking up girls."

"You think girls are easy now, try picking up guys."

I shook my head violently. "No, that's just way too much to assimilate for one day."

She just smiled. "There's time. Men are actually pretty satisfying. My first experience with that wasn't so hot, but the less said of that, the better. Nowadays, men are just so tame and cute you want to take them home."

I blinked. I didn't think I wanted more revelation of Ashley's frightening age right at the moment.

"And of course you can't get pregnant. Or venereal disease."

"What, I can't get sick?"

"You can't get sick. Not physically. Don't worry, though, there's plenty of scary stuff out there that can make you magically sick now."

"It couldn't before?"

"Well, no, before it would just have killed you, or annulled you."

I blinked. "Annulled me? What does that mean?"

She just looked at me. "You're a smart girl. What do you think I mean?"

I just laughed. "What, changed time so I'd never been in the first place or something?"

"You're quick."

I was utterly appalled. "Wait, really? I was just joking."

She walked on silently for a moment. I had just noticed we were back in the house when she said, "The world you see, the world we all see as intelligent apes with too much language facility for their own good, is almost entirely illusion. None of it is all that real, Violet. It turns out that what we imagine is reality. The fact that most people now imagine something pretty scientific and rational is more fortunate than you will be able to believe for some time.

"Ha. Time. A propos that." She threw herself down on the sofa and kicked off her shoes, and thought a minute. "In your case, I think this is going to be important, so listen closely. Time itself is an illusion, no more real than any of it – except that we have a really hard time seeing past that illusion, so it's a very persistent one. Really powerful magic users who start to see past time tend to ... not have been there, one day."

"They annull themselves?"

"They annull entire nations, babe. Just like Atlantis. It's gone. It never was, except Plato heard about it from somebody who'd been there. Like Pellucidar, when we realized the Earth had never been hollow. Hell, the Earth itself is smaller than it once was, although space certainly is bigger now."

"This is giving me a headache."

She just laughed and nodded. "Headaches, you can get. Ha. Speaking of headaches, how's your sexual urge?"

"Huh. I feel pretty normal, actually."

"Yeah," she nodded. "Your magic is waking up, starting to channel it. You'll still get horny more often than would be normal for a mundane, but you're not going to be nearly as desperate. I hope," she added, which kind of ruined the calming effect she was going for.

"Well," she went on. "What are we going to do with the rest of this beautiful day?"

I laughed. "I've heard that before! What do you want to do?"

"Ah, well, we can't do a whole lot, because you're probably going to get sleepy pretty quick; you're still recovering from the transition. But you want to go to the beach or something?"

"Wow," I said. "Knowing a teleport is going to be pretty nice!"

"You know it, girl!" She jumped up and bustled off upstairs, and came back with two bikini bottoms and a couple of towels.

"Uh, where exactly are the tops, Ashley?"

She waved a hand. "Pshaw. Where we're going you don't need a top, Violet. Just be happy I'm taking pity on you to the extent that you get a bottom, and change."

I shrugged, and followed instructions, then I took her hand and stepped through to ... I have no idea where, actually. The signs were in French, and it was late afternoon.

"Don't we need sunscreen or anything?"

She just looked at me as though I were an idiot, and spread the towels out and stretched out on one. "This is the perfect way to digest breakfast. Let's just nap in the sun."

And so we did, for a few hours. There were enough other beautiful women on the beach that we didn't attract undue attention, so I didn't suddenly turn invisible again, and we just talked about my childhood, mostly, and 80's movies and nothing much else. Not about magic. When I tried to ask questions, she just shushed me. "You've had enough for one day. Don't be in such a hurry. You have plenty of time to learn all you want." Boy, did I ever hope that wasn't foreshadowing.

She bought me a drink, and bought me some kind of crunchy ice cream concoction, and bought me crepes, and a hunk of delicious French bread with ham and cheese and shockingly wonderful tomatoes in it, and a candy bar, and another drink, and finally the sun started setting in what must have been the west.

Chapter 5

Claim Before the Storm

"LET'S HIT IT, BABE," SHE SAID, AND I WAS SO DROWSY I could hardly follow her. She ported us directly to my bedroom, so all I had to do was to fall over into bed. It was still afternoon here, but it didn't matter to me; Ashley drew the drapes and I knew nothing.

When I woke up, it was morning again, I was naked again, and there was plentiful sand in the bed from the previous day. I felt amazingly awake, as though the world were in focus for the first time in my life. I felt fantastic as I greeted the lovely girl in the mirror, noting that I hadn't really changed much since yesterday. Maybe my tits were a little larger, but it was hard to say. I was still stunning.

On impulse, I tried a couple of yoga postures I had learned a few years back. They were all effortless, and I could immediately sense that if I got any benefit from them at all, it would purely be in terms of concentration and symbolism. Physically, I was already literally perfect; I was as limber as a gymnast and strong as a weightlifter. I

want to say that it would take some getting used to –
except it wouldn't. I would never again pull a muscle, get
lower back pain, or fail to open a jar, after all. Perfection is
what we imagine for ourselves all the time; it's imperfec-
tion that takes getting used to, for everybody except magic
users. If you're magical, your self-image, perfect as it is, is
your physical body.

Maybe I could understand why evil witches were
supposed to be ugly. What if their self-image was full of
self-loathing and that was reflected in their outward
appearance?

The scary thing about magic is that it makes far too
much sense.

Not even bothering with the bathrobe, I wandered
around looking for Ashley, and finally found her in what
must have been her study.

"Oh, hey babe, did you sleep well?"

"Wonderfully." I looked around at all the books and
drawings scattered around.

"Hungry?"

I thought about it. "Actually, no. I feel great, though.
But not really hungry."

"Damn, you move fast." She laughed. "You're already
through your transition in, like, a week. You'll find you
don't actually get all that hungry, usually. Magic users
tend to glean energy from their environment anyway, and
it spills over into your metabolism. You'll only get hungry
when you wantto eat. More like entertainment."

"So the reason you only made bacon and eggs is..."

She giggled. "Yeah, it's pretty much all I know how to
make on a stove, and it's all the food I keep here on a

regular basis. As a teleport, I just step over to a good restaurant when I want to eat something. Which reminds me." She tossed me some keys, which I snagged out of the air without thinking. "Keys to the car, in case I'm away and you need to get out of the house."

"Thanks," I said with a frown. "I'll just put them in my pocket here." I gestured down at my naked body.

"Smartass. Just don't lose them." She rolled her eyes, but couldn't hide a grin. She really did like me, I guessed.

"What do you mean, 'make on a stove'?"

She looked exasperated. "How long do you think I had to cook before stoves were invented? I can make you anything that grows in this part of the Americas and can be made edible. You'd hate it, mind you, because most of the spices were still just growing where they later got found, but you wouldn't starve.

"Good thing, too. After I didn't die, I woke up stark naked in the middle of the forest that had grown where my last village had been. It was summer, luckily, or I would have had a much more miserable time of it, but I had to make my bone tools to sew some leather clothing before I could venture out into the world of man, for obvious reasons." She waved at herself.

I just shook my head in wonder. She just went down and down.

"So what are you studying here?" I asked, for lack of anything better to talk about.

"Oh, just answering some letters and wondering what I should show you that might not screw you up too bad," she replied. "Do you have any questions that you want to ask? The subconscious is good at highlighting the things you need to learn next."

I went over to a plush armchair with stacks of books on it, and carefully put the stacks on the floor before draping myself over the chair and swinging my bare legs in the air, jingling the car keys on their ring on my finger.

"I'm not sure, Ashley. It just all seems so inchoate and confusing so far."

She nodded. "Fair enough. That's probably because it is inchoate and confusing. Could I ask what your religion is? One thing's pretty universal, and that is that your religion will have a very formative impact on how you perceive and work with magic. Most of my early stuff involved my own people's gods, smoking odd weeds, and chants. I eventually moved beyond that, but it was very useful for a long time."

I blinked. "Religion? I'm agnostic, actually."

She pulled her lip. "Wow. That might be a first. I'm not even sure how to advise you – there's just no telling how you'll see the world behind the world."

I laughed. "So this reality is the world that's been pulled over your eyes?"

She looked blank. "The world that...? That sounds very good, actually."

"You've seen Highlander but not the Matrix?"

"Well," she said with some embarrassment, "I haven't been to the movies much recently. I was seeing a guy in the 80's that really liked popular film, but we ... parted ways."

I shook my head in mock outrage. "The Matrix is about a virtual world run by machines in which humanity is enslaved as a power source, and virtual reality is provided to keep them from finding out. That part's kind of lame, but the movie itself was fun." I frowned. "And not really that recent. I think I was twelve when it came out."

That got a genuine laugh from her. "You'd be surprised how quickly a decade can go when you have enough of them under your belt."

And that's when the roof caved in. The last I saw of her – for some time – she was battling what appeared to be a dragon by throwing lightning bolts, not that any of it was all that comprehensible to me as I was running headlong for the woods, naked as a jaybird and, I'm fairly certain, invisible. Certainly nobody was following or even looking my way, and I felt the same tight feeling in my chest as I had the previous day.

Of course, that could just have been fear.

The actual shooting was over pretty quickly, as far as I could tell, but the house was ablaze. I watched from some bushes for most of the day, marveling at how little it was bothering me to be naked in the bushes, and how lucky I was to be alive at all, and how much I hoped Ashley would show up and rescue me. The fire had still not gone out when I felt my daily sleepiness coming on; having no real choice, I curled up in a pile of leaves and slept.

Chapter 6

The Journey Alone

I WOKE UP FREEZING COLD IN THE MIDDLE OF THE night with a gasp and my heart trying to escape my chest, and it took me a minute to remember why. Oh, yeah, the only home I had in the world and my only means of support had just been fried by a dragon.

A freaking dragon. And here I was, not a stitch, nothing at all in the world except – oh. I had the keys to a car, still clutched tightly in my hand. And yeah, Ashley could teleport, right? Sure! So she had clearly escape and just couldn't get back, probably because there was a dragon here. I'd just have to do the obvious thing: get the hell out of Dodge and lie low for a little bit until Ashley could find me, or until I could figure out a little more about ... about things, and find her instead.

Trying to be as invisible as possible, I padded over the scorched grass to the house, with the vague idea of trying to find some salvageable clothing, but it was far, far too hot to approach, even if I'd had shoes on. I just hoped the car had survived the fire, or otherwise it was going to be a long, hungry, cold walk to someplace with people.

Searching around the perimeter of the house and jumping at every crack of the coals or whisper of breeze in the trees for fear it was a lurking dragon, I finally found the garage, thankfully a separate building. The car was fine, and turned out to be a DeLorean, of all things. Already feeling on a little more solid ground, I got in and adjusted the seat all the way forward so I could reach the pedals, and started the engine. It caught first try; Ashley may not have used it much, but she clearly kept it well-maintained. I checked the rear-view mirror – despite the fact that I'd just been in a dragon-battle-engendered house explosion slash fire and slept in leaves and dirt in the woods, my hair and face were perfect. I even looked like I had freshly-applied mascara on, and lip gloss. Freaking amazing.

Stomping on the accelerator, I purred out of the drive-way. Not a single rescue vehicle had arrived even now, hours after the fact, and I wondered how far the neighbors really did live. Maybe the house was magically hidden or something. Maybe nobody except magic users could find it. And dragons.

When I got to the main road, I eeny-meenied a direction and started driving as fast as the car would go. It was nearly dawn before I started to worry that I had no money for more gas, and in fact I was still naked, although oddly enough that didn't bother me that much. I think I was starting to feel, deep down, that social norms simply had no hold on me.

Finally I came to a town, which turned out to be

Knoxville, Tennessee . The sun was coming up, and I still felt mentally supercharged, more alert than I'd ever been. On impulse, I stopped at a gas station, with the vague idea of obtaining a map so I could do a little better than just driving in a random direction.

I had no better idea of how to proceed than simply to go in and ask for one, and so, squaring my now-insignificant shoulders, that's what I did, fear tightening my chest. There was a little diner area where a couple of truckers were eating breakfast, and a nice-looking lady running the cash register as I stepped in the door, the bell ringing. The lady looked over when the bell rang, then went back to her conversation with one of the truckers.

Not a single person seemed to notice or care that a stark naked beautiful girl had just walked into the store. I don't mind telling you that it really creeped me out.

Bare feet slipping a little on the floor, which had some mud on it from the heavy dew, I went over to the cashier, but somehow couldn't say a word again. Belatedly, I recognized the feeling. I was invisible again.

I heaved a sigh of relief. No wonder they didn't react - they weren't just unnaturally polite; they couldn't see me at all. Good thing, too! This being only the second time I'd ventured into the world in my newly shrunken frame, the truckers seemed the size of ogres.

Trying not to feel as though I were pushing my luck I grabbed a fork from the counter and helped myself to an egg and some sausage from the trucker at one end of the row. He was reading the paper and didn't even notice he'd lost some breakfast, but the warmth felt awfully good going down my throat.

It wouldn't do to get too comfortable or cocky, though, I realized. I didn't have a lot of practice with this whole invisibility magic thing, but it sure felt like I was only invisible as long as I was afraid of being seen. So I tried to feel afraid of being caught as I found the map rack and rifled through it for Tennessee and Kentucky candy and snack aisle - and slipped on the slick spot again, maps flying as I landed smack on my ass.

Nobody even looked. Gulping, I gathered up the maps, grabbed a bag of chips and a couple of Twix bars, and scurried back out to the car. Clearly the symbol of feminity thing could only cover me just to a certain extent. I didn't feel all that full of feminine grace.

Once back in the car, I checked the gas gauge. It was still on full. "Clearly," I said to nobody, "Ashley has modified this car a little." Well – one less worry! Then I pulled out the maps and figured out where I was. I had been driving away from the nearest larger city, but at least it wouldn't be too much further to get to Nashville.

And in fact, by noon, I had found a mall in Nashville and helped myself to some clothing, nobody the wiser. Surely any security cameras would notice a naked woman stealing clothing, but since nobody could find me, I was safe for now. I hoped. At any rate, there didn't seem to be much I could do about it, and I can tell you that social norms or not, it felt pretty good to stop being naked so I could be visible again.

I also collected a nice sleeping bag, so I wouldn't get too cold sleeping in the car. I was already feeling tired again; this transition thing sucked. Once back in the car, I drove a little ways out of town, found a nice secluded spot, and snuggled into my sleeping bag. One really nice thing about being small, I decided before falling asleep again, was that cars were suddenly sufficiently roomy for comfort.

I passed the night without incident. Sitting behind the wheel in the morning light and feeling pretty damned hungry, I tallied up my situation. I was a young-looking girl with no documentation at all, with a magic car that didn't need fuel or, I hoped for the long term, maintenance. I didn't seem to need to eat much, but I did need to eat some, I thought. I had to sleep a lot. I could turn invisible at will, and maybe I could do other magic as well. I had no money whatsoever, no belongings except the car, the clothes on my back, and a sleeping bag, and I had no job skills except programming. I was extremely good-looking.

So I did the obvious: I got a job that morning as salesperson in a comic book and game shop. I could talk the talk, and physical beauty was definitely in my favor. They got a good deal for hiring me for cash under the table paid on a daily basis, in return for my not showing them any documentation. I let them believe a nasty ex was out for vengeance and I had to stay low, and I told them my name was Charlotte. So sue me, it was the first thing I could think of, and I thought Ashley would counsel me against reusing the name "Violet".

Not having anything better to do, and since I didn't mind reading comic books all day when there were no customers around, I worked twelve hours every day, netting me the princely sum of three twenties folding cash. Bill, the owner, frequently remarked on how amazing it was that I still looked fresh and ready to go at the end of the day, and I had to admit I was needing less and less sleep as time went on. Of course, even if I were dead on my feet, I'd still look marvelous, I knew, but there was something about the safety and familiarity of the atmosphere in the shop that charged my batteries. It was good to be there. Also, the palpable sexual tension somehow lent me energy; maybe there was more succubus in my nature than Ashley had let on. Anyway, about half my money went for a motel room I rented for the week, but hey, I had a little folding cash, and I had a place in the world. I could even buy some more clothing and not rip anybody off.

It was obviously good for the shop, too, so everybody won. Girls are in short supply in the gaming/comics world, and a good-looking cashier who actually reads comics brings them in by the dozen. I think hiring me was the best thing that had ever happened to Bill, which is why it was really disappointing to come in one morning to find him talking heatedly with a guy who essentially radiated "cop". From what I could hear, somebody had clearly figured out I wasn't actually on the payroll, and somebody in the cop's office was determined to make an example.

I marched right up to them, seething with anger and trying not to show it; when I got up to him, I couldn't help but notice that I only came up to about the cop's collarbone.

"What's the problem here, officer?" I asked in my most chipper voice.

Bill and the cop both winced, but the cop didn't miss a beat. "Ah, you must be 'Charlotte'. We have reason to believe that you are an undocumented worker here. Can you show me some identification?"

Jokingly, I did a Jedi pass. "I'm not the undocumented worker you're looking for."

The cop blinked. "Oh, I'm sorry. You're not the undocumented worker I'm looking for."

Flabbergasted, I looked at Bill, whose jaw was on the floor. He looked at me in panic, and shrugged. Employment cops are generally not well-known for their senses of humor in situations involving their duties.

I did another Jedi pass. "Um, there's nothing here you need to worry about?"

The cop nodded, and said as though it had just occurred to him, "There's obviously nothing here I need to worry about."

Bill and I traded another look, and so I just did another pass, and in my best Ferris Buehler voice, said, "Have a nice day!"

"Well," said the cop, "Thanks for your time and sorry for the mixup. Have a nice day!"

And he left. Bill and I stood there looking after him, the he turned to me.

"What the living hell was that?" The look on his face was priceless.

I couldn't do anything but shrug. "All I know, Bill, is it's probably time for me to move on. Even if that guy actually believes what he just said, there's got to be paperwork that will bring somebody else back."

But he was just laughing. "Did you see that? Did you see that?" He was nearly doubled over now. "You just did a Jedi mind trick on that guy!"

His laughter was infectious. I couldn't help but giggle, too. He was waving his hands, saying "I'm not the undocumented worker you're looking for. Bwahahaha! I'm from Nashville. Your Jedi mind tricks don't work on me, only money! Hahaha!

"Shit, Charlotte," he said, opening the cash drawer, "I'm going to miss you, but you're probably right. The damn Stormtroopers always come back sooner or later. Here." He handed me two hundred bucks. "Consider it severance. Look us up if you're ever back in Nashville."

"Dude, I can't take this." I tried to push it back to him, but he shook his head.

"No way. You've brought in more business than this, easy, and you obviously don't have squat. I see how you wear the same clothes every third day. Take it, and be safe."

I nodded. "Thanks, Bill. I owe you one."

He just shook his head. "No. Just ... do something else, something Jedi, before you go, OK? This is already the best story I'll ever have to tell, and it would rock if it ends perfectly."

I shrugged, and did my best to imagine the cop coming back in the door and finding me. I knew I had it right when Bill's eyes bugged out just like Ashley's had, back in that diner. He actually looked around to be sure I hadn't, I don't know, ninja'ed over behind the racks or something, and then, quietly, like he was questioning his sanity, he said, "Char? Did you really just turn invisible?"

It wasn't easy, but I managed to lean over towards him and whisper, "Preciousssssss..." I left him laughing fit to die.

Knowing I might have to leave on short notice, I had

gotten into the habit of keeping all my meager list of possessions in the car, so I didn't even need to return to the motel to check out; I just hopped in the magic car, started it up, and pointed it west, pondering the questions of the day and – forgive me for neglecting to mention this – letting the car keep itself on the road.

Discovery the first: Jedi powers worked. Did that mean that any coherent magic system should serve to channel my energy? I decided that was probably so.

Discovery the second: my first "superpower", invisibility, came right after Ashley named me "Violet". Violet was the name of the daughter in The Incredibles, a shy teen whose power was ... invisibility. And, come to think of it, force bubbles. Imagining myself to be Violet, I held up my hands and tried to "keep stuff out". Sure enough, a bubble appeared. Maybe that had been some kind of subconscious association.

Discovery the third, or maybe just question the third: did Friend Stormtrooper have some connection to the dragonrider? Were they looking for me in some way? Did they have magic sniffers? Was my use of the car itself going to give me away – not that that was much of an issue, given that I'd just Jedi-mind-tricked their minion, if this was the case. Talk about a dead giveaway.

It was just about that time that I noticed that the airplane shadow I'd subconsciously seen paralleling the road flapped.

Shit.

I rolled down the window and looked straight up – sure enough. It was the dragon, or at least a dragon. So maybe it could smell me. In panic, I felt myself go invisible

– and that's when I saw the rider. And that's when the rider saw me.

Argh! Tolkien invisibility – not a barrier to dark forces! I had a wild idea, all of a sudden. If all the magic systems worked to structure reality, then what would a klatha drag-onrider lock look like? No sooner had I had the thought than a blazing dot of bluish-white light appeared in my head, tracing a complex figure; as it moved through the figure, I felt hotter and hotter, until abruptly I felt a silent click. I looked back up at the dragon, which was now looking around in confusion; the rider was trying to rein it back in and looking to a spot slightly behind me now.

I leaned down into the window and said, "Kitt! Speed up!" Well, of course I called it Kitt – what would you call a car that can follow instructions?

And that's when I had the most amazing idea in the entire world. I was in a DeLorean. Jumping back down into the driver's seat, I scrabbled in the glove compartment, finally finding what I was looking for – a pencil. Eight inches, pine with yellow paint, graphite core. What the hell? I waved it.

"Accio flux capacitor!", I stated clearly and calmly, and looked behind me to find the familiar trefoil shape. And sure enough, in front there was now the vintage control panel with the dates –– I carefully set the target date to three weeks prior, and accelerated to 88 MPH, then stopped the car quickly as the windshield frosted over.

Chapter 7

Back to Last Week

I JUMPED OUT AND LOOKED UP AT THE SKY. NO TRACE of dragons whatsoever. Heh.

It took us only a day and a half to get back to Ashley's house, since the car could drive at night while I slept. I wished I had known about the self-steering feature earlier, I grumbled. Once I got into the area, I had no idea where to go, but fortunately the car knew the way back to its own garage, and I just let it have its head. And presently, we rolled into the drive, and to my great relief, the house was still there, in perfect shape. I wondered when I'd gotten back, in terms of my transition – I was entirely unclear regarding how many nights and days had passed.

Then I felt an incredible blast of sexual energy radiating from an upstairs window, and knew more or less when it must have been. I had arrived during my two days of wet dreams, just before we went out to the diner. Good God, I thought. Ashley was right. This was way worse than snoring. Standing there looking up, I felt my uterus spasm with a partial orgasm, and felt moisture dripping down my leg. Yecch.

Heaving a sigh, I knocked ever so lightly on the door, hoping Ashley was a light sleeper. Sure enough, I saw a light come on where I figured her study must be; maybe her bedroom adjoined it. I hadn't actually seen her bedroom yet, I realized.

The porch light came on, and I squinted in the sudden glare as Ashley opened the door and stood gawking for a moment at me and the DeLorean, which was standing in the drive in front of the house with one wing open.

"Shit," she said. "Time travel?"

I nodded. "Time travel my way."

Suddenly she let loose with a guffaw. "I gave you the keys to the DeLorean, didn't I? Oh, Good Lord, I just never thought! It's going to be so freaking fun to have a young magic user around!" She waved me in. "Where are my manners? Come in, come in!"

Just then another wave of sex hit us, and she laughed at the look on my face. "You really are belting it out up there!"

I was mortified. "I used to snore and thought that was bad. This is way worse." The sexuality was building, and she leaned in and kissed me hard.

That was all I could take – I hadn't had sex in a couple of weeks, surrounded by testosterone-soaked gamers, and so I pushed her down on the couch and we went at it like bunnies for a little bit.

"Whew," she said afterwards. "That helped – it's been

over a day now and you're having a dream every half hour or so." She got up, and I noticed that her hair was still perfect and she was clean. It was the oddest effect.

"So," she said. "I still have some bacon and eggs if you're hungry."

"And how!" I said, and then suddenly realized that my showing up now was why we had to go to the diner in the morning. Huh. So the time loop was stable? Which meant that the future was inevitable now? Damn. She was going to die anyway, assuming she'd died at all.

She was bustling in the kitchen, and I told her to stop. "I'm a grown, transitioned girl and I can cook my own damn eggs. Sit down for once and let me cook."

She laughed. "Fine, suit yourself. But maybe you should also tell me why the visit?"

"Well," I started with a sigh, "In about... well. Tomorrow after I get up, I guess. A dragon is going to attack you. I think maybe you died. I had the DeLorean and ran north to Nashville, and holed up for a couple of weeks, but they found me and sent a government man in, and then the dragon with a rider."

She pulled her lip. "A dragon... with a rider? Mei Ling likes dragons, but her dragons would never accept a rider. I'm going to have to ask around a little. How did I fight it?"

"Lightning bolts." The food was done. "Do you want some?"

"Sure," she said, gesturing to the cabinet, which opened to allow two plates to float down. She didn't even notice she'd done it, and I chuckled to realize she was capable of a lot more magic than she'd let me see earlier.

"So it turns out I'm a Jedi knight," I said, dishing out the food.

Her face lit up. "Oh, that is priceless!"

"Also, my invisibility works like Tolkien's One Ring – dark forces can see me better when I'm invisible."

"Your what?"

"My ... oh, wait, that's tomorrow for you." I waved a hand at her. "You didn't hear me mention invisibility."

She almost spoke, then knitted her brows. "Damn. I was just about to ask what was tomorrow, but you just did a memory charm on me, didn't you?"

I gulped. I'd been joking, but magic doesn't know from humor. "Do you mind? I don't want to complicate the time loop more than I have to, and I told you too much."

"Huh," she said, and nodded. "That makes sense. Just ... don't make it a habit. I've got some failsafes that might trigger automatically if you erase too much, and I'd hate to have to scrape you off the walls."

My blood ran cold. I did have some habits to break. Suddenly I wasn't so hungry.

"Oh, dear," said Ashley. "You look like you've seen a ghost."

At dark o'clock in the morning, pitch black out, and knowing I was now capable of seeing ghosts, thatdidn't make my back crawl at all. No sirree!

"The dragon," I said, attempting to get back on track, "couldn't see me once I'd fashioned a klatha dragonrider lock."

She shrugged. "That's a system I don't know. Sounds like a target-specific cloaking mechanism, though. That's very promising! Very promising indeed, my friend."

We finished midnight breakfast in silence, then I got up to wash the plates and put them away.

"So what are your plans now?" she asked.

"I honestly have no idea, Ashley. I've just been reacting. I came back here and now to ask you what I should do next, and to warn you what was going to go down. What do you say I should do next?"

"Well, you still don't know much. You should probably stick with me."

I nodded. "I'll have to stay out of sight tomorrow so earlier me can have the day I remember. Otherwise, we'll be into a branching model of time and I'm not sure I can deal with that yet."

Ashley laughed. "Whatever. Time magic is the worst, so if you think you have a clue, you're the boss on that."

"I'll have to pull my copy of the DeLorean out of sight, too, so I can find the current one in the garage without being confused." I thought. "And the house is going to burn down. So rescue anything you'd miss."

Her eyebrows shot up and she sprang to her feet. "O-kay, thanks for mentioning that part! I guess I've got work to do."

"Can you copy the books and papers in your study? I saw them tomorrow morning."

"I can certainly fake it for you, don't worry."

With that, she was gone. I puttered around in the kitchen, cleaning it more than was necessary and wondering what to do with myself for the next day or so. The sky was getting light, so pretty soon I'd need to be out of sight of myself for the day.

First things first, I thought, and went out to tell Kitt to

hide off the side of the driveway in the woods where I wouldn't see him, driving out day after tomorrow after the fire. He closed his door and drove off, and as I turned back to the house, Ashley leaned out of the study window and called quietly, "Nice trick, kid!"

I just stared up at her. "What, I thought you'd added that feature. And, you know, the bottomless tank of gas?"

She grinned and shook her head. "Not me, babe. I have a mechanic keep it in shape just in case I need a quick non-magical getaway sometime. I don't even have a license. The last time I drove was in St. Louis, and I had to wear goggles and a scarf." She stared down the drive for a moment. "So much for the non-magical getaway aspect. Ha! Well, it's traditional to give your daughter a car when she reaches her majority, so – it's yours!" She closed the window with a final grin in my direction.

So all right, I'd also magicked the car to be a time-travelling Kitt that never needed gas, and hadn't even known it. Shaking my head, I went back up to Ashley's study. It was a whole lot messier than I'd seen it last. Or first. Whichever. Obviously she wasn't going to bother duplicating it entirely, just faking it enough to fool me.

"So Ashley," I said, "I'm stumbling over new powers and abilities on basically an hourly basis at this point. Where's the limit?"

She just looked at me sadly. "Limit? There are no limits, that's the problem with magic. The only limits are the ones placed on us by our own perceptual limitations and by other magic users – and that's only because if we imagine a reality that's too off the scale, they can't perceive it at all, so it's not ... as real.

"The problem with a consensus reality that is only real by consensus is that reality is pretty damned wacky." She went back to bundling documents; as she finished each bundle, it vanished, presumably to another study in another house somewhere in the world. She looked back up to me. "Insofar as there is a reality. Sometimes I wonder."

"Do," I swallowed, "Do magic users ever suffer from schizophrenia or anything?"

She just looked at me. "What do you think?"

"I'm starting to think it was really irresponsible of you to make me a magic user, that's what I think." I sank into the same chair I sat in day after tomorrow when the roof was going to cave in.

"So how many magic users are there, actually?" I asked.

She shrugged. "We don't actually know. It's ... complicated, counting us."

"What? How can it be complicated to count people? Do they hide?"

"Babe," she said exasperatedly, "Have you ever heard the saying, 'The universe is not only stranger than you imagine, it's stranger than you can imagine?'"

"Sure, you just told it to me, but I'd heard it before."

She sighed. "When did I ... let me guess. I haven't yet. My point, though, is that counting is already a rational act. The number of magic users is literally uncountable. Not as in 'infinite', but as in 'it's not actually a number'. I can't even know who is going to attack me. I've never heard of such a person, but you know what? They might never have existed for me yet. Seriously. Hell, for all I know, they're just your own projection of 'bad guys', and you yourself called them into existence by worrying about their existence."

"That ... that does seem frighteningly plausible, actually. That rider was awfully Tolkienesque."

"Whatever the hell that means," she grumbled quietly.

"JRR Tol–"

"No, babe, never mind, seriously, I don't have the time right now. Let's just agree that you're the expert in Tollhouse magic."

Mm. Tollhouse magic sounded pretty good. I'll bet if I clapped my hands and believed in cookies very hard, I could do some Tollhouse magic. I did so, even clenching my fists, but ... no such luck. There was something I was missing.

Oh, hey! There was a pencil on the desk! Six and a half inches, pine, graphite core – pretty close to my specs. I picked it up and waved it. "Accio cookies."

There they were. I ate one, and offered one to Ashley, who ate it gratefully, apparently with no notion whatsoever of the irony.

"So why do I need a wand to make things appear?"

She ate another cookie and shrugged. "Damn if I know. Ask your therapist. We all have our little self-imposed limitations, though. I think it's inherent in human psychology to require some sort of grounding – which given that fact that the universe demands no such limitation, is probably the only reason we've survived, once we reached the symbol manipulation stage of our evolution."

"Did we actually evolve? I mean, everything's up for grabs at this point, right?"

"Ha. Well, that's a good point. Now we actually

evolved. A couple of thousand years ago, though, we arose from formless void in a dozen different ways. It's ..." She waggled her fingers.

"Stranger than I can imagine, yeah," I nodded.

"Take my teleportation. The reason I can teleport myself and other things I'm touching is that fundamentally, there's no such thing as distance or space; these are simply constructs we agree upon. But I can't perceive that absence of space; my brain is simply built to see space. And in fact, our construct is so consistent that we can describe it mathematically."

"Wait!" I said. "I always thought it was suspicious that mathematics manages to describe physical reality so neatly!"

She nodded. "Exactly. Humanity has imposed that math on the world recently. If you made the same measurements three hundred years ago, before the math was applied, you may not have gotten the same results. Or who knows? Maybe you would have! But it's still a basic truth that I and others like me have discovered that the mathematics of physics are optional."

I looked at the sky outside, which was now full-on morning. "If you want to make sure this morning happens the way I remember it, Ashley, you need to go upstairs, get undressed, and get in bed with me."

She raised her eyebrows. "Ooh. That sounds rather nice!" She stood up and wriggled out of her clothes right there, striking a pose.

"Good God, Ashley." I squirmed in the chair. "With all the rest of this, I often forget how damn lucky I am you walked into that store."

She smiled and kissed me long and hard. "Later today, after you've gone back to sleep upstairs, let's have a little private time, shall we?"

"Definitely. Definitely."

She sashayed out, leaving me hot and bothered. So I did the obvious: I tossed my clothes on the floor and did some self-exploration, which was fun and fulfilling. Then I had another cookie and walked around looking at her books.

I had to smile when she burst back into the room and threw her clothes back on, then looked over at me and grabbed my clothes from the floor, too. Then she blew me a kiss, and ran back out. To go to the diner for another breakfast, I remembered. So far, so good – no disturbance of my past. I had to laugh at the realization that I'd ended up buying the clothes I wore to the diner and hadn't even noticed the resemblance.

I was back in the chair, feet propped up on a stool and reading a fascinating little list of ancient European magic systems, when she came back in to hunt for bikinis and towels. I'd Accio'd a plate of French fries with ketchup and a Coke. Magic use might be hazardous to your sanity, but it most definitely had its perks.

Incidentally, if you're a Potterite, I've learned this isn't the way Accio works. I got it wrong from memory; it's a summoning charm, not a creation charm. That was a little surprising, and even more surprising was that, having found this out, it still didn't harm my ability to Accio nonexistent items into existence. Once the brain has seen something happen, it doesn't matter much what the source material originally said.

"Violet," she said from the closet, "I can't find my bikinis."

I grabbed my pencil. "Accio beach stuff."

"Thanks, babe!" And she was gone.

I just kicked my bare feet some more and read. Took a little nap just to freshen my brain, only to wake up again to a kiss.

"Mm," I said. "Your mouth tastes like crepes."

She smiled. "You know, I've always known I had a permanent glamor, but it's something else entirely to see it on somebody else. You are just fine, girl."

"Likewise, darling," I said. "Accio crepe. Yum."

I took an overly-large bite of the crepe, and talked around it while Ashley slouched in her desk chair, bare feet up on the desk. "So let me (wow, this really is good), let me get this straight."

I chewed while I thought, and managed to swallow. "Basically, then, you're saying that the fundamental struc-ture of the universe is whatever people believe it to be?"

"Yup," she nodded. "In fact, it's even worse than that. It's whatever people can believe it to be."

I swallowed my next bite. "Meaning....?"

"Heh. Meaning that you don't have to fundamentally believe something to be true for it to manifest as reality. You can just fear it might be true, or hope it might be true, or will it to be true."

I crammed the rest of the crepe into my mouth, chewed, and swallowed. "So what you're saying is that ... well, wait. Is fiction that I've read now true?"

She blinked. "You know, I hadn't thought of that. I checked my list of magic users I personally know to exist, and the last one created - again that I know of - was over two hundred years ago. Fiction wasn't all that popular yet. Classics, sure. But fiction? You kids today have tons more than..." Her brain started to catch up with what she was saying.

I swallowed, my mouth suddenly dry. "Ashley?"

"Yeah?" She looked wary.

"Ashley, what you're telling me is that there is a slight but finite chance that every fiction I have ever read could now be part of our actual physical reality, right now."

She didn't say anything.

"And that might have still been safe, if you'd found somebody ..."

"If I'd found somebody boring?" She was smiling gently.

I nodded wildly. "You, however, found a wild magic user who grew up in a mundane society knowing at some level that he was meant for greater things, and our society has a lot of literature for dreamers like that."

Holy crap. I'd thought dragons were going to be a problem? I sprang to my feet, unable to think fast enough.

"Ashley, I am insanely grateful that you gave me this chance to be pretty and all, and I think - no, I know - that I love you more than I ever thought it was possible to love a human being, but do you have any idea the stuff I like to read?"

"You really love me?"

I screeched to a halt (something deep inside was gibbering Kzinti, Klingons, and zombies, oh my! Nick Cage's sun storm, John Cusack's crustal instability, megapiranha vs. Godzilla, there were a million ways for everybody to die, and mutant powers, Moon Nazis...) and I looked at her. Her face was heartbreaking. I nodded. "Yeah, Ashley. I really do."

She brushed a tear from her eye. "That's the nicest thing anybody's said to me in a really long time."

"Ashley, I think my mind is going to destroy the world."

Chapter 8

Finding a Minion

SHE WAVED A HAND AND LOOKED AT ME LIKE A kindergarten teacher looks at her favorite, though somewhat slow, pupil. "Oh, dear little Violet. Do you really think the rest of us could comprehend all the doomsday scenarios you dream of? The Earth cannot die unless all of us grow to believe in these events, or die."

I blinked. Checks and balances. "And you're immortal."

She smiled ruefully. "So far, yes. As are you."

"And independent of thought."

"Ha! Yes, pathologically so."

I sat back down. "So Galacticus can't eat the Earth."

Her laugh was musical. "No, whoever Galacticus is, he might try, but the Earth is safe. He can't destroy it any more than Ragnarok could destroy it."

"But Ragnarok hasn't happened yet!"

"Ah, you've heard of it? Yes, now it hasn't happened

yet. But when it happened earlier, before the Gods became myth, the Earth abided, and now it never happened at all."

I thought. "Like Atlantis?"

"Like Atlantis. Now shoo, I have to finish packing up before your dragon shows up to burn this house down."

I'd actually managed to forget that little detail what with all my doomsday panic, and I jumped to my feet again. "The dragon! Ashley! How long did I sleep this time?"

She looked up from the papers, vaguely. "Now how would I know that? I'm still in your past, my love. But your transition is almost over, so it could be tonight."

"It was morning. There was still sand in the bed from the beach, so almost certainly tomorrow morning. Oh, hell."

"What?"

"It's been a couple of weeks and a lot of trauma for me, but I think there's no way we could have had the conversation I remember after having the conversion we just had."

She shrugged. "So?"

"So if it's not a closed loop I don't know what time travel will do to us. I came here in a Back to the Future DeLorean and I don't want either of us to fade out of existence."

"Dear, I have already created you. Marty McFly inadvertently prevented his own conception."

"Yes!" I nodded vigorously. "OK, well, we didn't have much time to talk before the roof caved in, so ... I guess, just ask me about my religion and that should be close enough."

"What is your religion, incidentally? I meant to ask earlier. Your religion will have a very formative impact on how you perceive and work with magic. Most of my own-"

"Ashley!"

"Yes?"

"Save it for tomorrow morning, this is exactly what you asked me then."

She pulled a face. "I told you I hate time travel." She went back to packing, seemingly without a care in the world.

I looked out the window. It was about noon. The other me wouldn't wake up until tomorrow morning, I didn't want to distract Ashley's preparations any more, and for the life of me I couldn't imagine how I could prepare for a dragon.

I Accio'd up a comfortable hiking outfit consisting of sturdy boots, comfortable underwear, and a nice blouse with a midlength loose skirt, put it all on, and stuck my pencil/wand in a convenient wand pocket I'd visualized in the skirt. I suppose slacks of some kind would have been a little more normal for hiking in the wood, but even after a couple of weeks it still gave me a kick to be girly, and after all I couldn't really get scratched, so I figured I might as well enjoy the added mobility of a skirt and bare legs.

Then I chose a direction at random and set off into the woods surrounding Ashley's house, just kind of letting my mind wander a little and assimilate the crazy world I'd been plunged into.

After about an hour, I felt almost relaxed again, and I realized that it would really help if I could consult some reference material about the magic systems in books I'd read.

I needed a library.

Unfortunately, it would take hours to get to a decent one by car. Dammit, I thought, pinching the bridge of my nose, I could see the F/SF stacks back in Paris.

On the next step, my foot fell not on crunchy forest floor but on carpet. Startled, I took my hand from my eyes and looked around at ... the F/SF stacks back in Paris.

"Of course", I said to myself. Teleporting to a library would work just like that. Feeling a little weak in the knees, I wandered over to a chair and relaxed into it, letting the library ambiance wash over me like ... like a very relaxing thing.

The next thing I knew, a gentle hand was shaking me awake.

"Miss?"

I startled just a little too much, not too surprising given my recent life, and the librarian jumped back as I rocketed to my feet, breathing hard.

"Oh, I'm sorry, dear." She furrowed her brow. "Are you all right? It's just that we're closing, and you've been dead to the world all day. Do you ... do you have anywhere to go?" She put a hand on my arm, very warmly.

I took a deep, shuddering breath and let it out. "Oh! Sorry, I guess I was a lot more tired than I thought. Don't worry, I'm fine." I smiled at her and she relaxed visibly, smiling back. She was maybe in her early 40's, obviously worked out, didn't think much of makeup.

"Good," she said. "I've been watching you all day,

wondering where you got that leaf mold on your boots. And you don't have a purse or a pack or anything. Do you need a place to stay, dear? You're not in trouble, are you?"

You have no idea. "Trouble? No! Things were just a little tense at home and I wandered over here to do some reading, and I guess I just slept all day!" I managed not to laugh hysterically, wondering how she'd react if I told her I came to do some research on a dragon that I knew was going to attack my home because I'd come from the future to warn Ashley.

She saw it. I realized I knew her, vaguely. I may have mentioned that as a guy I'd had a difficult time interacting with my fellow humans. For some reason I'd lost the shyness when I became a girl. She'd always been friendly to me, even though I'd never so much as looked her in the eye back then.

I answered her skeptical look with a grin. "You wouldn't believe it anyway. Trust me."

She grinned right back. "Kid, I'm a librarian. Let's go get something to eat, if you want. Then you can hit me with your best shot. But I just did the sweeping up, and you tracked in a trail of forest mulch and mud when you entered the library, and from that trail, you entered the library in the middle of the stacks."

Nobody ever noticed that level of detail when Davey did it. I pinched the bridge of my nose again. "And you've read Jumper, I take it."

She didn't say anything, but when I dropped my hand and looked at her, I surprised the most amazing hungry look before she blinked and straightened up.

I sighed. There must be an awful lot of people made to apprehend the true magic and strangeness of the world; maybe we all yearned for more than our mundane consensus reality? In a sense, these were my people.

"So yeah," I ended up saying. "The world is stranger than you imagine."

"I can imagine a lot." She walked into the back room, I assumed to get her purse and things, and I followed.

"So can I, and that's kind of the problem." I watched her fish some keys out of her purse and we went back out into the library. We were the only ones left in the place, and she ... "What's your name, actually?" I asked.

"Kathy." She turned out the lights and shooed me out the door, then turned around to lock up. "What's yours?"

"I'm told it's not a good idea to tell people. You can make something up if you like."

"O-kay... I'll call you, um... I can't actually think of anything."

I laughed. "Maybe later."

"My car's right over there. Do you have anywhere you'd like to eat?" She unlocked the car and got in, then unlocked the passenger side door for me and I opened it.

"It's all good. Pick someplace you like. I'll buy." I sat into the car, slightly confused about how to arrange my skirt as I sat. Also I noticed that my wand pocket had been poorly designed for sitting; the pencil stuck into my thigh and I gave a little yelp and squirmed as I pulled it out of my pocket.

She blinked. "With what? I still don't see a purse. That's why I thought to offer you a meal in the first place. What's wrong with your skirt?" She seemed a little alarmed at my awkwardness, perhaps only now realizing she was alone in the car with a possibly crazy person, and I couldn't think of a graceful place to put the pencil.

After starting the car and pulling out of the parking lot, she said, "Why did you just pull a pencil out of your pocket? And where did you get a skirt with a pencil pocket, did you make it yourself?"

"Yes, actually. And it's not a pencil, OK?" And if that didn't convince her I was a crazy person, what would?

She snorted. "Yeah, I'm pretty sure it's a pencil."

I nodded. "In a sense, it's a pencil. It was on a desk when I picked it up. But it's also eight inches of pine, yellow paint, with a graphite core."

She looked over at me. "What?"

"Acciomoney," I said, and waved the pencil. "Where do you want to eat?"

She did a classic double-take at the small pile of twenties on her dashboard. "Where did that come from?"

I just showed her the pencil. That shut her up, and we drove in silence until we got to a nice Greek place I knew well, and pulled into its parking lot.

After we got out, she just stood there a minute, then turned to me and said, "So where did you learn that trick?"

"No trick, actually. And that's the problem."

She gestured towards the door of the place. "You have a Harry Potter wand in the form of a pencil and you can use it, and that's a problem?"

"No, the problem is that apparently anything I've ever read shapes the way the world works for me."

"And by shapes the way the world works, you mean..."

We picked a booth and sat down, and I held up a

finger to stop her for a moment. "I'm going to try something here."

How would a klatha privacy shield work? Just a lock, I guess, and Captain Pausert was always good at locks. I thought about it, and just as before, I saw a sort of ultraviolet point in my mind's eye that traced a complicated curve until I heard a click and the air around us became abruptly foggy for a brief instant, then cleared.

Kathy jumped. "What did you just do?"

"Well, I tried to put a privacy shield on us so people don't overhear what we're talking about."

"But how did you make that foggy look?"

I just looked at her.

"You're serious, aren't you?" She looked like she couldn't decide whether to run screaming, laugh hysterically, or jump up and down clapping. She compromised by just bouncing up and down in the seat a little.

I couldn't help but smile. "Yeah. It's kind of cool, right?"

"But if this was the first time you tried it, we should test the shield, right?" She jumped up and went over to the next table, then sat down. "Say something."

"Wow, Kathy, this is a good idea! I'll just say some stuff now. OK, you can come back."

She just sat there barely containing her glee, then moved back over and sat down in the booth again. "That was cool! You looked perfectly normal, and you said some stuff, and as soon as you said it, I couldn't remember a word of it! I could only barely remember I'd told you to do this!"

I laughed. "Heck of a lot easier than doing Jedi passes on everybody in here!"

Her eyes got even wider. "Jedi... Really?"

I just nodded. "I've actually done it, twice. I was just joking both times, but it worked."

She hugged herself like a five-year-old on Christmas. "Damn. How did this happen?"

So I told her the whole nine yards, all of it, from meeting to Ashley to the dragon to time travel to worrying about all the things that I might make happen. She stopped me a couple of times with stuff like, "So wait, you're a guy?" and "Klatha like the Witches of Karres? I love those!" and especially "But Accio couldn't create a flux capacitor that didn't exist already!" but overall she listened and let me talk it out, and in a couple of moments cry it out.

It was surprising what a relief it was, talking to somebody who understood. And amazingly, Kathy actually did understand, perfectly.

By the time I was done explaining, it was in the wee hours and we were walking through one of the little state parks on the lake north of town, looking at the moon, just a day or two past full and quite beautiful. We'd wound down into a comfortable silence.

"So..." Kathy paused. "So we could go to the moon. Right now."

I nodded. "I guess so. I'm not sure how to do it."

"If what you're telling me is true, we could get there in a chariot pulled by geese."

"If I understand it, some people could do that, but I can't because for me it's a vacuum."

"So the Greys could take us in their flying saucer."

"I guess."

She looked at me in the moonlight. "You're worried about Ashley."

I sat down on the damp ground. "Kathy, I can't handle this. This is above my pay grade. I have no idea how to help her, or even what happened tomorrow morning."

She sat beside me and put an arm around my shoulders. "Aah, come on. Think back a little and talk to me about it."

"I don't actually remember much. I'm pretty sure Ashley had the dragon well in hand; she was shooting lightning bolts at it and it seemed to be working, and then I turned and ran and after that she was gone."

"Well, it's not your fault, turning and running from a fire when you're buck naked. Really the problem is that Ashley disappeared. We just need to trace her, because she teleported away and then didn't come back. Maybe she was hurt."

"Burning does hurt her, yes, we established that. And my biggest worry is that she just burned to nothing and won't be back for centuries, but it's more probable that she teleported out. But how can we trace her? Give her something? I wasn't there tomorrow morning - or rather, earlier me was, but this me wasn't."

"So you have until earlier you wakes up. It's about 3 now - plenty of time!"

I took a breath and blew it out. "Yeah. Thanks, Kathy. I just feel lost with all this and you're a real help."

She punched me on the arm. "Ah, come on. What are minions for?"

I had to grin at that. "You're my minion now?"

She nodded decisively. "Yeah. You bet I am. I've lived my whole life for this day." She got up, groaning a little, then held out a hand. "Come on, get up. Maybe Ashley herself can help."

I let her help me up, and ineffectually slapped at the wet stain on my skirt. "What's that Rowling charm for cleaning up?"

"Scourgify?"

I pulled out my pencil and waved . "Scourgify." Both our clothes were perfect again.

"Nice!" She looked down at her own clothing. "Even the coffee stain is gone!"

I smiled and held out my hand, and she took it, looking excited. And then we were in Ashley's kitchen. Kathy gleed a little, looking like a kid at Christmas yet again. Hand still in hers, I led her up the stairs to Ashley's study, which was looking much, much emptier now. Ashley wasn't in evidence.

"Darn," I said. "She's not here."

"She'll be back," Kathy said, and just as she did, Ashley reappeared behind her desk, smiling as she saw us.

"Ah, you're back!" She came around to give me a hug and a kiss, then turned to Kathy. "And you have your first minion!" She looked like a proud mother.

I felt myself blush, thinking this was more than a little disrespectful of Kathy, but Kathy seemed to take it as it was intended, and held out a hand. "Kathy Barnes. Pleased to meet you, ma'am."

Ashley walked around her in a circle, then looked her directly in the eye. "Nice pick, my flower. Kathy, you are quite powerful in your own right, and now I sense my Violet's force moving through you as well. I have no doubt you've yearned for something your whole life, something you sensed was there that no-one else noticed." She licked her thumb and pressed it against Kathy's forehead. "Now you have it. Use it well."

She looked at me. "I sense you need something from me. I really have to run and finish something, but what is it?"

"Tomorrow morning - this morning - you're going to battle the dragon and disappear. I'm worried you'll have been burned and unable to return, so Kathy suggested that I have something to track you through teleports so we can come to you if necessary. But I don't know how to start. Can you help?"

She nodded. "Yes. Good idea." She vanished momentarily, then reappeared with a ... well, I guess a talisman on a chain. "This can find me wherever I am; I infused it years ago with my own essence by wearing it for over a hundred years."

Kathy gasped, very quietly, and Ashley chuckled. "We do live a while, Kathy. You'll have your own chance to see, soon enough." She looked at me. "I have to go. I'll be back in the morning before your other self comes down, but my errand can't wait. Hide in the woods or further away, and be safe. You'll find me or I'll find you, babe. Don't worry. And Kathy will be a good help to you now."

And she was gone, just like that.

I put the talisman on, letting it hang down into my blouse between my breasts, which was a very odd feeling indeed. But comforting. I really felt like Ashley was in it; I suppose in a real sense she was, and it made me feel warm and safer.

I turned to Kathy and looked at her forehead. "I wonder what that was about."

She made a little air-blowing noise. "I don't know, but as soon as she did it, my knees stopped hurting. And they've been hurting for three years now." Her shoulders drooped. "I feel exhausted, though. We've been going all evening and night without stopping, and I'm no spring chicken, my girl. I need a little nap before our friend the dragon makes an appearance."

"Well, this house is gigantic and there's no shortage of bedrooms in it, so let's find one. I feel totally wired after sleeping all day, so I'll make sure you don't oversleep."

So that's what we did. I knew which wing not to go into, because I was already asleep in it, but there was a very comfortable room not far from the study that even had some comfy sleepwear in it for unexpected guests. Kathy stripped down right in front of me to put on a voluminous shirt. She was amazingly buff for a forty-year-old, and I had to gulp.

She turned around and smiled at me, oblivious. "Whew, it's good to get out of those clothes after a long day." She climbed into bed and closed her eyes. "Oh, this is the best bed I've ever felt. I'm in love with this bed. I gotta...."

She was asleep. I pulled the cover over her a little. Asleep, she looked a lot younger, the little wrinkles on her forehead and around her eyes smoothing out.

The room had a comfortable loveseat with a reading lamp, so I kicked off my boots and socks and folded my legs up under me. "Accio Harry Potter Cliff notes." Nothing like a little boning up on some of the magic systems I did more or less know. "Accio Witches of Karres."

I read for about an hour, and noticed I was getting pretty drowsy myself. Ridiculous, how much I was still sleeping. I had the vague notion that I got sleepy when I discovered new magic for myself, so surely it would eventually level off.

"Accio alarm clock," I said, and set it for seven. That should be safe. Two hours should definitely help. I pulled off my clothes, leaving only Ashley's tracker amulet, which was going nowhere without me, and climbed into bed next to Kathy, leaving the light on so I wouldn't sleep too deeply, hopefully.

I looked at her face, so relaxed and looking even younger. Apparently she'd really been tired.

Next thing I knew, the alarm clock was ringing and there was predawn twilight infusing the room. I did, in fact, feel much better. I looked over at Kathy, but she wasn't there.

I sat up, rubbing my eyes, and the door to the en suite bathroom opened, and Kathy backed out, still wearing her nightshirt and still looking at the mirror inside.

"Dude," she said, "Come here. You gotta see this."

I sprang out of bed, alarmed. Now what? I looked in at the mirror, and saw two pretty girls. One was me, and the other was definitely Kathy - but looking about eighteen and with a distinctly unsettled look on her face.

"Ah," I said. "Ashley must have made sure that as a good minion, you'll last."

She nodded. "So it would seem, Boss."

I scowled at her in the mirror, but she just smirked and said, "Well, you just don't look like a Violet to me, and I have to call you something, so that's what I'm going to call you. Ashley's right about the names having power thing, and 'Boss' is more a title than a name. I'll be damned if I'm going to contribute to anybody having power over you. So I hope that's OK with you, Boss."

She looked at me. "Wow, you're even cuter naked."

I could feel myself blushing again. "Sorry. I'll get dressed."

She raised an eyebrow, but didn't say anything. I pulled on my panties and started buttoning the blouse before I noticed she was still watching me.

"What?"

"I think maybe Ashley did more than just make me young," she said.

I rolled my eyes. "She could have asked."

She shrugged. "I dunno. I don't think I mind, actually. Do you, um, do you like girls?"

I nodded.

She looked down at her own clothes, which she was holding in her hand. "Well, that makes things a little easier. So here's my problem this morning. I've dropped at least three dress sizes and my tits are smaller, too. Not to mention I think I'm a little shorter. None of this stuff is going to fit me. Are there clothes somewhere in this house?"

I picked up my pencil and she smiled.

"Let's try something," I said. "Ashley said you had

power of your own and that my power is flowing through you." I handed her the pencil. "Go ahead."

Her eyes got very, very wide. "Seriously? You're serious. Oh, Lord." She waved the pencil at herself. "Wingardium leviosa."

If it were possible for someone to die of geekgasm, Kathy would have been a corpse five times over by now. She floated up off the floor, weightless and giggling, and I couldn't help but smile. She looked at me, now upside down. "You know, we really need broomsticks if we're going to be serious." She started swimming through the air, using a breaststroke.

I held out my hand for the pencil and she did a graceful sumersault to hand it to me. She looked like an astronaut in the ISS except her hair and clothes were always in perfect order and hanging down, for her current temporary down.

"Accio Kathy's wand." A new pencil was in my other hand, and I flipped it over to her. "Acciobroomsticks." I stepped into my skirt, then pulled on my socks and shoes, and picked up one of the broomsticks. I thought a minute, forming an image carefully in my mind. "Accioarm holster."

A little wand holster appeared, strapped to my lower arm. Way more comfortable than the pocket in my skirt. I stuck the pencil into it, then tested the other feature - with a little flip of my arm and a little practice, I could easily pop the pencil out of the holster into my hand. I ran through it a couple of times. If I had to to be limited by my preconceptions and needed a wand to focus my Accio work, I wanted to be limited as little as possible.

"OK," I said, looking up at Kathy. "Ready as I'm going to be. Breakfast in the kitchen when you're ready for it."

She was practicing walking on the ceiling, but the Wingardium was wearing off, I think; her hair was hanging down towards the floor and her nightshirt couldn't make up its mind which direction was up, either. Pretty soon it was going to start getting revealing.

I laughed, teleported to the kitchen, and Accio'd a full breakfast spread, from Nutella to the perfect hash browns, and dug in. Presently Kathy showed up, broom in hand and with clothing remarkably similar to mine, right down to the wand holster. I think she'd imprinted on me.

She ate with as much gusto as I did. "Oh, man," she said. "It's great to be young again. You forget how wonderful it is to eat." She showed me her arm. "This holster is a great idea. Just like Colonel Bayard, right?"

"The little slug gun!" I knew it came from somewhere. "If we live through all this, we've got to go looking for Zero-Zero Stockholm and the Imperium."

She nodded enthusiastically. "I personally want to meet Sherlock Holmes."

We went on in that vein for a while, periodically whipping up more food, until finally we had to admit that there just wasn't any more room inside us. Kathy used her wand to flip away all the dishes, and, brooms in hand, we left the house and flew up into the air as the sun was rising.

"Kathy," I said, "I want to fly a holding pattern and see if we can see where the dragon comes from."

She nodded. "Makes sense. Accio binoculars." She tossed a pair to me. "A girl could get used to magic use."

I grinned and widened my eyes at her in agreement,

and we commenced searching. Kathy had a tendency to loop-the-loop that I found really stomach-turning.

I was really starting to enjoy the morning when she suddenly screamed. I turned to see her torso falling to the ground, and the freaking dragon, obviously teleported in from nowhere, grinning at me, Kathy's leg still sticking out of its mouth, until it opened up, crunched horribly, and swallowed.

I admit it. I gave in to the hate. With a primal scream that surely broke windows in Tennessee, I launched myself at it, Palpantineque lightning shooting from my fists. The dragon was already smoking when we crashed through the roof right into Ashley's study. I had a brief glimpse of my earlier self, naked and glorious and an arm thrown over her eyes in protection, as we crashed on through the floor. Just as I saw her, she vanished, clearly having gone invisible in order to run.

Ashley jumped down after me and the dragon swivelled its head towards her. Most of the house was already in flames at this point, and the dragon wasn't looking so good; my lightning had vaporized one wing and it was bleeding profusely from one side. It still had plenty of energy to take a deep breath, though, and the flame that came out wasn't flame - it was plasma. Ashley had just enough time to throw me a panicky look before she was gone.

I can't really remember what came after that; I essentially blacked out for a few minutes, but when I came to, there was nothing left of the dragon but charred meat and glowing embers, and I stumbled out into the back lawn to find Kathy's remains.

And found her. The dragon had eaten everything below the navel, and she'd broken her neck in the fall. Devastated, I gathered her up in my arms, and teleported to the only safe place left to me that I could think of - my old apartment back in Paris. I wouldn't owe rent for another couple of weeks, after all. Once there, I set Kathy down on the arm chair and collapsed on the futon, exhausted, and cried myself to sleep.

Chapter 9

Finding Ashley

I woke incredibly refreshed to the smell of breakfast, sunshine streaming in the window, a tray with one of those metal plate covers at my side, and my head pillowed on a supporting arm.

It wasn't enough to keep me from yelling and jumping to my feet on the futon, of course, which woke Kathy up. She smiled lovingly up at me, her eyes still a little crossed and squinting in the sunshine.

"Well!" She scratched her cheek as I boggled. "You're looking better!"

"But you-" I collapsed back to my knees next to her, looking in her eyes.

"Ah, what kind of a minion would I be if I up and died on you?"

"But your neck was broken!"

"I got better!" She didn't do a really good Monty Python accent, but it was a good try. "Apparently Ashley

90

wanted you have a really reliable minion, for which I am incredibly grateful."

"But the dragon ate your butt!"

"Ah. Well, here's the thing," she said, and threw the blanket back.

"Gaaah!" I jumped back. She still only went down to about an inch below the navel. The rest of her was missing. "But how--?"

She shrugged and sat up. "I'm pretty sure it's magic."

I realized there was no way she should be able to sit up. "How ... what are you sitting on?"

"Remember that one Niven short story about the guy with the psi arm?"

"What? Oh. Yeah, he had telekinetic powers but he could only use them through his missing ..."

"That's the one. My body image seems pretty set." She got up, torso hanging in midair at just the right height. "Here's the really funny part, though." She walked ... floated ... over to the chair and pulled on some slacks there, then pulled on socks. And looked entirely normal, except for an inch or two of missing midriff in between.

I just goggled at her for a minute. She grinned and took off the pants again, leaving her socks incongrously standing on the floor under her levitating torso.

"So," I cleared my throat. "So you're invisible from the waist down?"

"Kind of." She waved a hand under herself; it went right through. Then she turned around and walked through the chair; the socks stayed behind as her virtual body went on through. "That part took a little practice. I can kind of choose whether to manifest more solidly or not, otherwise I guess I'd keep falling through the floor." She came over and sat on the futon next to me again, presumably cross-legged, although it was impossible to be sure.

I reached out a hand and touched her side, then moved it down her hip, which I could feel perfectly. "Your index of refraction is bang-on the same as air." Then I pushed through her to the surface of the futon. I could choose, too.

"It's not refracting at all, Boss. I checked. It's just as invisible in water."

"What? When?"

"I woke up two days ago; you've been conked out all this time. I kind of wonder if it's not your power doing this healing for me, actually."

"You've just been waiting here?"

"Nah, I've been walking around town, and I went up and got my car and drove it back here. I'm not even sure why. My driver's license doesn't look like me any ..." She smacked her face. "Aaand, it only now occurred to me that I could just make a new license."

"Or a new car."

She left her hand over her face. "Ugh. Magic. It just isn't easy to assimilate."

"Tell me about it." I looked over at the food. "So how long has that been there?"

"I just made it and I was going to eat it myself if you didn't wake up again. Then I laid down a little and ended up falling asleep again. Hungry?"

"And how!" I pulled the tray over and set it on the

futon between us, and ate and ate. Kathy ate a little, but not all that much.

"What's up, aren't you hungry?"

"I lost over half my muscle mass a couple of days ago; there's less to feed."

I nodded. "That's logical. But probably only true because you believe it."

She shrugged. "Don't worry, anyway, I'm fine." She ate another strawberry and laid back on the pillows and watched me finish up.

Finally full, I put the tray back over off the futon and snuggled into her arm again with a sigh. "I can't tell you how glad I am you're alive."

"You and me both, Boss." She was watching my face closely, and suddenly I realized why, and it made me tingly in interesting places.

I cleared my throat again. "I look pretty good now, don't I? With the whole magic glamor thing?"

She nodded cautiously.

"And before, you weren't, you didn't..."

She shook her head and raised an eyebrow. "But I have to tell you, Boss, that I sure do like girls now. At least one girl. Walking around town, I've been testing it. I don't really feel any attraction for anybody else out there. None of them compares to you anyway - not just physically, but your being is, is, well, singular somehow."

I was definitely getting warmer in the places I didn't use to have. "This worries me, Kathy. It feels like I'm taking advantage of you."

She nodded. "I know what you mean, Boss, and all I can say is that inside, in my core, I know that I have only existed, my entire life, for you to take advantage of me, if you see what I mean. I've always been yours, I just didn't know it yet. I feel as though I was literally put on this planet to be yours. And I'm totally OK with that. I was OK with that from the moment I saw you in the library. It's like I've finally found the team I've always wanted to play for."

This whole thing was making me unbelievably horny, and I knew without a doubt that she knew it. The bond between us was palpable, not to mention that my nipples were hard enough to draw blood against her side.

"Kathy?"

She grinned. "Yeah, Boss?"

"Ashley says people who have sex are stronger." I gulped, unable to think of anything I wanted more right at that moment.

"Well, then I guess my duty is clear, Boss." She gently disengaged her arm from me. Heart pounding, I felt her move slowly down to my crotch, teasing. "By the way, I figured out a really neat trick with my body image I think you'll like."

I wasn't really processing at a verbal level, so I just moaned. She opened up my legs and I could feel something warm and hard up against my labia, then gently pressing into them, between them and on, very strangely, into me, filling me up. My mind exploded, and I'm pretty sure I screamed in pleasure, which afterwards seemed kind of embarrassing. A glass on the counter exploded, then the television.

I didn't care, I just wanted more of whatever was happening to keep happening. I opened up my legs even more, and confusedly perceived Kathy's torso floating over me, her hands on my legs and a bemused look on her face. Now the thing inside me felt like it was moving back and forth, and every slight movement caused more and more intense pleasure. My hands went involuntarily to my clitoris, and grasped an invisible shaft moving in and out of me.

Even through the waves of orgasmic pleasure, even as the windows burst outwards and I heard the screech of a car on the street outside as its windshield presumably self-destructed, even as a crack spread across the ceiling and the sun dimmed outside, even as the earth's crust started buckling in time with my spasms, I suddenly realized what Kathy had meant about her body image, and I laughed in delighted joy, wrapping my arms and legs around Kathy and doing my damndest to pull her bodily up into me.

How simple! Just like that Chalker novel, at the end, what was that? Messiah's Choice? Kathy would know, she probably copied it out of that one anyway.

With a final scream, I climaxed for good and collapsed on the futon, then waved a hand. "Reparo everything," I mumbled, and heard a rush of tinkling as all the glass reassembled itself and the dust swirled back into the plaster ceiling. The sunlight coming in the window brightened.

I just lay there for a minute or two, utterly at ease with myself and the world, then languidly turned my head and gave Kathy an unfocussed smile. She was grinning back, sitting in the chair, invisible legs up over its arm. "So I gather you liked that OK, Boss? I got it from Chalker." She shook her head. "I guess for you, the earth really does move."

I laughed. "Yeah, Kathy. I liked it." I took a deep breath and blew it out. "I feel like I could whip another dragon right now. Let's go find Ashley, shall we?"

I sprang up and quickly got dressed. A quick Scourgifygot all the ashes and charred spots out of my clothes and they were good as new. Kathy also pulled on clothes, which was hilarious to watch.

I wasn't joking. I felt ten times as powerful now. "Did you realize I just did that Reparo without a wand?"

Kathy nodded. "Yeah. So about finding Ashley, I had a couple of ideas and checked them at the library while you were still asleep. I didn't want to try anything without you, though. You are, after all, the Boss."

I smiled. "Thanks, Kathy!" I pulled out the amulet, still around my neck, and held it in my hand. "There's only one thing. Earlier, I could feel Ashley through this thing, and now it just feels like jewelry."

She shrugged. "So she'll reincarnate again later. We have a time machine."

"Wow! You're right!" I hugged her. "You are the best thing that ever happened to me."

"Second best, surely."

"Best, second best, whatever. Shut up."

"Yes, Boss." She hugged back. "The other idea, just in case she's still here in the present, is a scrying bowl."

"Oh, ho! English magic!"

"Right, straight from Jonathan Strange and Mr Norrell, which I read yesterday just to be safe. It looks pretty simple. I bought a silver bowl yesterday, just in case an Accio'd bowl wouldn't have the same silver magic." She picked up a plastic bag and pulled out a bowl, handing it to me.

"Good thinking. Where's my pencil? Oh, here it is, in my holster still." I flipped into into my hand, and went into the kitchen nook to fill the bowl. Then I brought it back out and set it on the table. I waved Kathy over, and used the pencil to draw quarters over the bowl. Faint lines appeared, sort of engraved on the surface of the water, which was an interesting effect.

"We're not interested in Faerie, and we're thinking about the whole Earth, not just England, so I'm going to modify it, OK?"

She nodded. "The book doesn't mention any actual words or incantations. If we want to really get into Strange/Norrell magic, I think we'd have to Accio Norrell's library and spend a lot of time with it."

"Ugh." I rolled my eyes. "Leave that to the English magicians. We Americans do things more directly."

She giggled.

"OK, so the quadrants are by hemispheres, north-east, north-west, south-east, and south-west," I said, touching each in turn. Nothing happened. I tried again. Nothing.

"Damn." I crossed my arms.

"Try something else, something you know exists."

"Man, you are a good minion. OK. Bill's comic shop. Same quadrants." I touched each in turn, and north-west flashed in a color I couldn't describe, one I'd never seen before. Sort of a greenish purple, really.

I blinked. "That was weird."

Kathy laughed. "It flashed in octarine, didn't it?"

"Ha! Yeah, I guess it did. You saw it?"

"Sure. This stuff gets easier when you wake up one morning, not dead, with an immaterial ass, and you realize you're not in Kansas any... Well, I guess we are in Kansas, but Kansas itself isn't in Kansas anymore."

I touched the quadrants again, saying, "US, Canada, Latin America, Caribbean," and the first quadrant flashed. "Northwest, Southwest, Midwest, East." The Midwest flashed.

I crossed my arms again. "So it works, clearly. Let's try the regular 'show us' thing. Did the book describe that at all?"

She shook her head. "Nope, just swirl your wand over it and focus on what you want to see. It's reportedly lousy for determining location because it's just a local view, but maybe we can see what's what."

I said, "Show us Ashley," and swirled the pencil over the bowl. The quadrant lines disappeared, and swirls of fog appeared within the water. I couldn't make anything out at first, but suddenly, just like those Magic Eye things with the 3D dolphins, I realized I was looking at a pile of smoking ashes and some flyblown chunks of meat. Large chunks of meat.

"That sure looks like what's left of Ashley's house," I said.

"What? Oh! Now I see, wow, that's a weird effect."

We looked at the smoldering coals a little while. They were still glowing after a couple of days. That had been one heck of a fire.

Finally I stirred up the water and the view disappeared.

"Kathy, I can only assume Ashley was vaporized and will reincarnate there at some point, just like last time."

She looked at me and nodded. "Yup. It's time for time travel!" She took the bowl into the kitchen and dumped it, then returned with it clutched under her arm.

I held out my hand, she took it, and we stepped into Ashley's yard, where the stench of burned, rotting dragon was indescribable.

"Oh, dear God!" I cried. "That's horrible."

Kathy strapped a gas mask onto my head and things got a lot better quickly.

I hugged her again. "Thanks."

"No problem, Boss. Where's the DeLorean?"

"Right over here, off the road where I wouldn't see it." I led her over to the spot, and Kitt started his engine when he saw us.

"Its engine just started, Boss. Did it ... see us?"

I nodded.

She grinned again. "Just when you think it can't get any better. He's a Transformer, isn't he?"

Yes. The urge to believe that was irresistable. "Kitt," I said, "Are you?" But I knew the answer.

"Yes, Boss," he said, unfolding into a vaguely humanoid form about twelve feet in height. He drew a sword and knelt before me, holding it out to me while bowing his head.

I looked at Kathy, and she widened her eyes and nodded towards the sword. Feeling faint, I picked it up - it was heavy, although as it was eight feet long it had to be titanium or something because it wasn't that heavy - and clumsily touched his shoulders with it. "I accept your fealty, Sir Kitt, and thank you for it."

He looked at me, eyes flashing. "I pledge my oath to thee, Boss, and death unto your enemies." He took the sword back and drew himself up to his full height. "Who shall we kill today?"

I smiled. "Well, today is a relative term. First, we have a time search to do. Back to DeLorean form, please."

"Yes, Boss." He folded up in an unbelievably wonderful manner and I was tempted just to have him transform and untransform all day long with a lounge chair and drinks, except then we'd have to take the gas masks off.

I got in on the driver's side, and Kathy on the other. Closing the doors, we pulled off the masks and chucked them back behind the seats. Kitt had a great ventilation system, apparently. I pulled the talisman out and held it in my fist. "So I'm thinking I might be able to use this as a detector."

She nodded. "If you don't feel her presence in one time, she's not there yet."

I slumped. "But if we do find her, and bring her back to today, then I'll just find her today."

"Hmm. That's a bit of a conundrum. I was going to say that we could just ask ourselves, but then we must have foundher, and so they wouldn't know either."

"Well, I know time travel works, though, because I already did it."

"I'm not saying it doesn't, Boss. I'm just saying maybe it's weirder than we can imagine."

I pulled my lip. I looked at the date on the flux capacitor panel, and set it for three weeks in the future, then lifted the car up (having long since decided that this was the flying DeLorean, not the boring old roadbound one) and revved it up to 88. With a flash, everything looked pretty much the same, and I circled back around to the ashes of the house. The smoke had gone out, and something seemed to have eaten most of the dragon; there were some really large bones.

Kathy looked over at me. "It flies."

"Yeah. Where we're going, we don't need roads. Cher, what could have eaten my dragon corpse?" I set Kitt down and got out.

She opened her door, but sat there a moment. "What does the amulet say?"

I grasped it. "She's not here yet." I waved her out, and when she was in the clear, said, "Kitt, transform." Whatever could eat a dragon corpse seemed a lot less scary when I had a twelve-foot metal warrior behind me sworn to kill my enemies.

We poked around a bit, but there was nothing. Kathy wordlessly pointed to some huge toothmarks on some of the bones. But everything was quiet.

After a while, I sighed. "Must have been another dragon, don't you think?"

Kathy nodded. "And it's gone, I think."

"Looks like it. OK, Kitt, let's search on."

He folded up and popped his wings, and we got in.

"Last time Ashley was fried, she's not sure how long she was out," I said. "It might have been a millenium or two. But we might want to try a binary search."

"Ah," said Kitt, and both Kathy and I jumped. I'd

forgotten he had a speaker in the cab, which was stupid of me. "Jump to the end of the search period, then halfway, then up or down a quarter depending on whether you detect her presence or not, and so on. That would work, Boss."

"Right!" Damn, I had good minions. "Can you just set that up? I'll say 'yes' if I detect her, 'no' if I don't."

"Program set up, Boss. Execute on 'Find Ashley'."

Kathy and I grinned at each other. "You should have called him Gay Deceiver," she said.

"Actually," said Kitt, "I do like that name a lot."

"But you're a guy, Kitt," I said. Then I thought about it. "Aren't you?"

"I don't have a gender per se. Would you rather I were a guy?"

I shrugged. "Not really. Do you want to officially change teams and take the name of Gay Deceiver?"

"I would like that, Boss." Her voice was suddenly different, a friendly, warm contralto. I couldn't wait to see her humanoid form.

"All right, Gay." I took the talisman into my hand. "Find Ashley."

We accelerated to 88 and -ulp- we were floating weightless, stars all around and the sun a blazing glare in the black sky. Air was hissing out of the car and pain stabbed my ears as Kathy let out a strangled and dwindling cry. "Gay, Bug Out!" I managed to gasp, and bam, we were flying over Ashley's ex-house again.

I rolled down a window a crack and air screamed back in at speed. Kathy's ears were bleeding. I felt mine, and it was the same. I flipped out my wand for a Reparo eardrum and felt them pop.

"Well, crap," said Kathy. "The Earth is gone in two thousand years."

I nodded. "Yeah, but I felt Ashley. Gay, can you transform into something airproof?"

"Sure, Boss. You'll have to get out first, though. It's pretty hard transforming with passengers."

"Logical. Set us down and do the trick, then."

"Roger, Boss!" She swooped down to a neat landing and we got out.

Sure enough, her humanoid form was different. Not terribly different - it wasn't really all that humaniform to start with - but it was softer, more rounded, daintier somehow, while still being twelve feet of deadly titanium killer machine. No sooner had she assumed that form than she had folded back down into something ... well, she had wheels and she had wings, and she was clearly space-capable.

Kathy said, "That looks like Heinlein actually described the Gay Deceiver."

"Yee-up. I think my sense of wonder is burning out, Kathy."

"I wonder if she has the annex in Oz and the never-ending basket of fruit."

"It's possible. Very possible."

"Are you guys getting in or not?" Gay's voice came from her wing speakers.

I stepped to the port hatch and knocked shave and a hair cut, and it opened.

"Cute, Boss."

"How did you know, Gay?"

"I don't know, Boss. It just seemed obvious."

"OK," I said, "Second time's a charm. We already checked two thousand years, let's resume from one thousand." I took the amulet in my hand again.

Gay dogged her hatches and lifted, then jumped. No Earth, no gravity, no Ashley. "No."

Jump. "Yes!"

Jump. "Yes." Jump. "No." And so on, the numbers narrowing in on the year 3370.

"Jump back an hour, Gay." Blip.

Kathy looked out the windshield. "Now what?"

"I dunno. I got the feeling Ashley thought the amulet could point me in the right direction, but I don't know how."

"We're weightless. If the amulet has an affinity to her, maybe there will be a slight attraction."

I shrugged. "Worth trying. Gay, jump us forward an hour again." I took the amulet off its chain and placed it in the air in front of me, and Kathy and I held our breath.

The amulet just hung there, tumbling gently.

"Gay, is this the right time?"

"Not quite, actually. Sorry, Boss. Time coming up in three, two, one, mark."

Nothing. We stared at it.

I heaved a sigh.

Kathy squinted at it. "It stopped tumbling, didn't it?"

I felt a silly smile on my face. "I think it did. Gay, can you tumble us, slowly?"

"Sure thing." The starfield outside slowly turned around us, and the amulet visibly moved with it.

"Which direction is which, girls?"

Gay said, "Towards the clasp. It's the distinguishing feature."

Kathy cleared her throat. "Away from the clasp. It's meant to be worn on the neck and would naturally spring away towards the target."

I snorted. "Fat lot of help you are. I still have to cast the deciding vote. I think Kathy's right. Gay, put the clasp to our rudder and ahead slow."

Of course, while we accelerated, the amulet fell backwards, so I caught it. After a short burn, when we fell free again, I put it back out in front of us so we could check bearings. It held steady for a while.

"Hey, Gay," I said suddenly. "Can you make a screen here on the panel where you can show us a face? I may be just a primitive primate, but I'd like to be able to see you."

"Inshallah, ya sayyid." A few seconds of complicated movement later, there was a screen about a foot square, and a smiling animated face in it. "How's that?" Her lips didn't move with the words very well, but the facial expressions were right on.

"Much better. Thanks! It's easier to think of you as a person this way."

She smiled warmly. "Thanks, Boss."

Just about then, the amulet suddenly swung around to point behind us.

"Gay, I read that as triangulating on a point that wasn't too far off. Can you do the math for me?"

"Roger, Boss. She must be about a mile off the port stern now, but without another bearing I can't tell in which radial direction she lies."

"Take us about. Back to free fall when you need more bearings." I grabbed the amulet before she fired jets.

It took two more bearings, but ten minutes later, there was Ashley right outside the windshield, blue in the face and unconscious, but definitely in the flesh.

"Do we have an airlock?"

"Sorry, Boss," said Gay. "I didn't think of it."

I moved my seat all the way back, then held my breath while I teleported right out to Ashley, took her in my arms, and teleported us both back into the seat. Neither of us was very big, so it was a tight fit, but by no means impossible.

"Oh," said Gay. "I didn't think of that, either," and Kathy and I cracked up.

"Take us back to Ashley's, Gay, then you can transform back into a car and we can head over to Paris so Ashley can recuperate in a safe place." And just like that, Earth was ahead. It was beautiful, so beautiful.

And doomed.

Chapter 10

The Uncertain Future

BACK IN TENNESSEE, WE LAID ASHLEY GENTLY IN THE bedroom to recover, and rigged up a screen in the apartment for Gay, who naturally had to wait out in the parking lot in DeLorean form - although she had quietly informed me that she thought of herself more as a late-model Volkswagen, and I had a strong impression that the next time I saw her she wouldn't be a DeLorean any more. By "rig up", of course, I mean "Accio video intercom for Gay", which accomplished the same thing. Any sufficiently advanced magic is indistinguishable from technology, and a lot of my magic was turning out to be the deus-ex-machina manufacture of magic objects.

Once Gay was "inside", Kathy and I snuggled up on the futon and the three of us watched some movies. I figured I was due a day or two off; the world wasn't going to end for a couple of weeks for sure - I'd been that far forward on foot, after all.

I think it was after Primer but before Time Bandits that the subject of our recent time search came up.

"I still don't get one thing," said Kathy. "If we picked up Ashley right when she reinstantiated, how coud the amulet detect her at a later date?"

"I didn't want to ask about it," said Gay. "I'm already impossible and I don't want to push the envelope."

I put my hands behind my head and preened. "Girls, that's why I'm the Boss. I just decided that since the universe seems to be based on narrative, I would consider time to flow in narrative order because it's the only way it makes sense."

Kathy just looked at me. "Boss, that doesn't actually make sense."

I shrugged. "Does to me."

Kathy and Gay looked at each other. Gay was getting more human by the minute.

"Well," she said, "It did work. We did find Ashley."

Kathy nodded.

Then we started up Time Bandits, which made even less sense than our search for Ashley, but hey, midgets. I kept falling asleep, feeling warm and safe surrounded by the best minions ever.

The sun was setting by the time I was forced to admit that Ashley wasn't waking up. Was, in fact, in what we figured had to be a coma.

"Kathy," I said, "What do we know about healing magic?"

"Sheesh, Boss, healing magic is all over the place. Are you a healer?"

"Why not?" I put a hand on Ashley's forehead and said, "Heal!"

She jerked and moaned, but didn't wake up. I looked at Kathy. "There is just no way that should have done anything."

"Yeah," she smiled ruefully, "But that's true of all your powers, right? It's when you least expect something to work that it seems to work best. I mean, Jedi mind tricks? When you were just joking?"

"Logically, I should be able to reach into her head and just grok what's wrong."

"Well, the classics are the best, and this healing wouldn't have been beyond Valentine Michael Smith, would it?"

"Thou art God, Kathy." I looked at Ashley again, and put my hands on her face in a Vulcan mind meld position. I'm not sure why; it just felt right. Sure enough, once I did it, I could see her brain perfectly, intuit where things should have been and where they actually were. And sure enough, there was hypoxia damage to a lot of the little blood vessels and neurons. I gently breathed order and logic back into them, and was rewarded by another moan from Ashley, and suddenly I was bowled over by her powerful memory of waking up in a vacuum, naked, sunburning on one side of her body and no way to breathe, and all that after being vaporized by a dragon a subjective instant ago.

I jerked back from her so hard I hit my head on the wall, leaving a dent. In the wall, not in my head.

"Whoa, Boss! What was that?"

I shook my head to clear it; I was seeing spots. "Maybe

the mind meld was a bad idea. Waking up in a vacuum wasn't a happy fun time for Ashley."

"But it looks like you did it!"

Sure enough, Ashley was awake and looking at me, brows knit and faintly frowning.

"Violet, is that you? Babe, you, I ..." She fell asleep again, this time hopefully actual sleep and not further coma. Kathy and I left the room quietly and gently closed the door to a crack.

"So it worked?" Gay was frustrated with her inability to move the screen around the apartment.

"It worked. She woke up, then she fell asleep," Kathy said.

Something new occurred to me. "Gay, isn't your humanoid form bigger than the DeLorean?"

"Yeah," she said. "So?"

"And isn't your roadable form as Gay Deceiver bigger than your humanoid form?"

She nodded from the screen.

"And didn't you strongly imply that you were going to try a VW form?"

She shrugged. "I already am a VW, Boss. I hope that's OK?"

"But a VW is actually smaller than a DeLorean, Gay."

"Where exactly are you going with this, Boss?"

Kathy had a thoughtful look on her face.

I sighed. "Sorry, Gay, the problem with making up the universe as you go along is sometimes you have to retcon some stuff as you think harder about it. You're obviously folding part of yourself outside our three dimensions."

"Well naturally," she said. "There's no way to rotate

joints to go from a car to a twelve-foot robot if you're restricted to three dimensions. It doesn't even make sense. And yeah, I never extrude all of myself into the three spatial dimensions. I'm actually very large."

"So there's no real reason your humanoid form has to be twelve feet tall."

She just stared at me from the intercom.

"You could just as well be, say, five foot eight," I said. "Right, Gay?"

She scowled, and there was a knock at the door. "Get the door, Boss."

Kathy walked over and opened the door, and Gay v2.0 walked in.

"What do you think?" She pirouetted. She essentially looked entirely human, if a little plastic in complexion and with the sexual characteristics of a lifesize Barbie doll. Her face was perfect, though.

"Wow, Gay," I said. "Be honest. You've been working on that face for a while, haven't you."

She smiled shyly. "Yeah. Since you first asked me for a screen out in space to make it easier to think of me as a person. That was really kind of you."

"Accio minion clothes," said Kathy, and handed Gay an outfit.

"Oh, don't worry," said Gay. "I can't wear those anyway because I couldn't really transform then and I don't want to leave the Boss unprotected. I have holographic projectors to project the appearance of clothing as needed, but I'm working on some ideas for textile extrusions that would let me transform realistically, clothes and all." There was a brief shimmer, and she was wearing a jumpsuit.

Kathy pouted. "No minion skirts?"

"No," Gay grinned. "Tight clothing only until I figure out textiles. Skirts that go through furniture are a dead giveaway."

"So are legs, Gay. Doesn't stop me!" But she was smiling.

"Girls," I said, "I'm feeling hungry and tired; it's been a long day even if a lot of it was spent lounging. Who's up for pizza and bed?"

Kathy held up her hand, and Gay said, "I'd like to try a bed."

"Kathy, whip up a pizza. I'm bushed and have no power of imagination left to me."

"We could just call one in, Boss."

Gay smiled. "I have just done so."

I just shook my head. "She's also a telephone."

There was a knock on the door and Gay's smile turned into a wider grin. "I'm also a time machine, Boss."

"Kathy, go pay for our pizza while I cower under the covers here, OK?"

"You got it, Boss! Accio forty bucks!"

The pizza was excellent and the delivery guy was ecstatic about the massive tip, and eating in bed isn't a problem if you can Scourgifythe crumbs and sauce away at will. Magic may be a gigantic pain in the ass, but it does make mundane problems go away.

Soon, belly nice and full, I went to sleep with Kathy on one side and Gay on the other. Gay obviously didn't sleep, but she said she felt more secure knowing nobody could possibly get to me without going through her, and I had to admit it gave me a warm feeling, too. Also her heating elements helped.

Just before falling asleep, I startled awake and looked at Gay.

"What is it, Boss?"

I held a hand out and Kathy put a pencil in it. "Accio light saber. Gay, I present you with this weapon. Use it wisely."

Kathy sighed happily. "You're the best boss ever," she said, but I was already asleep.

In the morning - well, early afternoon - when I finally woke up, it was to a dejected little band. Ashley was sitting in the chair facing me. Kathy was propped against a wall, arms crossed. I realized she really didn't need to sit down because virtual legs couldn't get tired. No muscles meant no lactic acid fatigue. Gay was in bed with me, and it was her arm I was using as a pillow.

I felt massively relaxed, so it was disappointing to see Ashley's face. Her expression was horrible, as though it she'd seen the end of the world.

In all fairness, she had.

She lit up when she saw I was awake, though. "My flower! Good, ah, morning."

Without moving a muscle, I said, "Morning, Ashley. Welcome back to the living."

It was obviously the wrong thing to say, and they all sort of clammed up.

"So... What did I miss?" I looked from one face to the next; none of them met my eye.

Ashley cleared her throat. "It's ... not easy to say, dear. I seem to have lost my magic." She looked at me, and for the first time since I'd known her, she looked old. Not outwardly, not yet, but there had been a vital liveliness in her eyes that was gone.

I sat up. "Lost it? I'd really like to be flippant here, like did we check between the sofa cushions, but I'm getting a bad vibe. How can you lose your magic? You're a magical creature!"

She nodded. "I'm a magical creature and my magic is bound to the Earth. It's just part of my formative experiences, I suppose. But when I awoke, the Earth was gone. And I felt a spark go out of me. Then I passed out, and woke up here. Kathy and Gay tell me you saved me, twice."

"Ashley, I..." I felt lost. I'd put so much faith in being able to have Ashley as a teacher. "I don't know what to say. What can I do?"

Her hair was black now. I wasn't sure when exactly it had changed. Had it been black when I woke up? "Little one, precious Violet, there is nothing you can do. I am fully a woman now, my outward form is all I am. And I am no virgin as a woman. I am merely a baseline human, not even enough power to make you a good minion."

"But you still know so much!"

She was already shaking her head. "You'll see what I mean, but no. Magic knowledge is itself magic. I know what I knew, but I no longer know the essence of it. With magic, the map is the territory; write it down and you capture only its outward form, but not the thing itself. And the traces in physical neurons are just another form of writing."

Eyes blurring, I managed to say, "But Ashley, I need

you with me!" I wiped the tears away and saw that not only her eyes were old; she herself was aging by the second. Leaping out of bed, I hugged her, trying to push my power into her, willing her to stay with me, but I could feel the vitality slipping out of her.

"Violet," she whispered. "Believe me, I'm ready. Be good, you and your stalwart friends." She kissed me on the forehead, and then she was gone. I was hugging air with a faint swirl of dust in it that vanished even as I watched.

I cried for a while, while Kathy and Gay sat next to me looking miserable. Presently, I'd cried it all out for now. "Damn her eyes," I said, "I didn't need a Kung Fu Panda kind of ancient master, I needed an actual teacher."

Kathy shrugged. "Boss, I don't think she could comprehend your style of magic anyway. I do, but only because the world has become the one I've lived in my head all my life. She wouldn't have been much help."

I tried to hit her then, but Gay's reflexes are literally inhuman and she wisely stopped me. Kathy didn't even flinch. I cried some more, then I sighed.

"Sorry, Cher."

"Apology accepted, Boss. I get it, really I do." She put an arm around my shoulders and I bonked my head against her. "But you don't need a teacher."

I nodded, face muffled in her blouse. "I know. She told me so herself. I still needed her."

Gay shook her head and I looked around at her. "No, Boss. You don't need anybody. Not really. Anything, anybody you need, you will shape the world to create - you created me whole cloth out of an old car, and I think you love me all the same, right?"

I took her hand. "Well, sure I do, Gay."

She smiled. "You love me because I'm part of you, Boss. I don't want to be harsh, but magic users are the ultimate solipsists. The world really does revolve around them. Around you. In a way, I think you magic users are the only people that truly exist. Ashley knew that. The Ashley you brought back was only a reflection of the true Ashley - she died with the Earth."

"Phew." I blew out a breath. "This is too much for me right now. For the last week, I've done nothing but lurch from one Ashley-related disaster to the next, and now we need to find out what's going to happen to the Earth, and I'm just too frazzled to think."

Kathy said, "We should take a walk or something."

I shrugged. "Where?"

"The Amazon? Mount Fuji?"

Gay said, "The Moon," and Kathy's eyes lit up.

She whipped her head around to me. "Oh, can we, can we?"

An involuntary smile started spreading over my face. I nodded. "You guys are the best minions ever. Gay, let's go to the Moon.

Chapter 11

Brace for Impact

AND SO WE ACCIO'D TWO SPACE SUITS AND GAY helped us put them on, then we all ran out into the parking lot and Gay transformed, and off we went. After a quick takeoff into the skies over Paris, Gay sighted the Moon and did a translation, and there we were, in lunar orbit, with a fading hiss as Gay bled the air out of the cabin in preparation for landing.

"Hey, Boss," said Gay, "Since when can I teleport?"

"Since I forgot you couldn't, Gay. Your namesake in Number of the Beast could; that's what the whole novel was about in the first place."

Kathy bounced in her seat. "Can we walk at Tranquility Base?"

"Sure, Kathy, as long as you Scourgifyyour tracks. It's a historic site, you know."

"OK, Mom."

"Does anybody here actually know where Tranquility is, though?" I looked at Kathy and at Gay's smiling visage on her screen. They both shook their heads and I shrugged.

"Let's just set down over there," I said, pointing at a relatively flat spot. "Someplace where we can see the Earth on the horizon so it'll look the biggest."

And just like that, we were down. Gay popped her hatches and we got out, then Gay transformed and stood between us and we watched the Earth for a while. It was astounding to see it.

Kathy broke the silence. "Weren't we going to actually hike a little, though? What's over there?"

"Inky black shadow," I said. "And a lot of dust." But I followed her over there anyway, and we walked down into a little valley and an attractive cliff face, with a sparkling granite effect that was really nice.

"Oh, hey, look at this," she said in a strangled voice.

There were footprints down there. Of course we had to follow them. And found graffiti. Leonardo da Vinci's signature.

"Oh, come on," I said. "I can't even remember where I read that, but now apparently I'll never again get to see anything without my own preconceptions messing it all up."

Kathy was just laughing. "Boss, you need to read some less fantastic stuff."

Still grumbling, I turned my back on Leonardo's scrawl and the rest of the walk was actually pretty nice; the Earth would poke out behind a ridge and we'd get Gay to save the image for later in lieu of an actual camera.

"I already record everything anyway," she said. "All you'd have to do is just ask me for pictures later."

"It's traditional to take the pictures while you're sight-seeing, not pick them out of a continuous record later," I said. "It's part of the fun. Oh, look at that crystal!"

A few hours later, we were back in Gay and up in lunar orbit again. "Swing around Farside, Gay. It'd be cool to be out of the sight of the Earth for a minute."

Kathy started to say something, then stopped herself, and it all crashed down on me again.

I sighed. "While there's still an Earth to be out of the sight of, anyway."

"I'm just simulating a real orbit by translating repeatedly along it, Boss," Gay said. "We haven't got all day."

"Well, actually, you're a time machine, so... Oh, God dammit." I folded my arms across my chest.

"What?" Kathy looked around. "Oh."

"Gay, see that big building over there?"

"What, the big hooked cross thingy? What about it?"

"Yeah, don't let them see us. Just ... wait a minute. Acciocloaking device. Gay, feel that new circuitry?"

"Yep. OK, we're cloaked, Boss."

Kathy laughed. "Yeah, it wouldn't do to get noticed by the Moon Nazis before they're ready to attack, right?"

"Let's ... let's just get back to Earth. I got a bad feeling about this."

"No, no, no, Boss," said Kathy. "Bad feelings are bad."

I didn't say anything, and Kathy and Gay traded looks.

"Next stop, the blue marble, Boss," said Gay. "Any particular place?"

"Low Earth Orbit, Gay." And there we were.

"So we know the Earth is gone a thousand years from now, right?" I looked at my motley crew. They nodded.

"We need to pin down a date. Gay, do a binary search. Your reaction ..." The Earth had flickered in and out for about a tenth of a second, and now it was there, but entirely red with lava.

I halfheartedly went on, "... speed..." and then wound down.

"I'd tell you to sit down, Boss, but -"

"Jesus, Gay, just tell me."

"Next month."

"Fuck."

Kathy reached over and took my hand. "Maybe we can prevent it. The future's not set in stone, right?"

I smiled weakly at her. "No. I guess it's not. Gay Pretender, take us home."

"Aye, aye, Cap'n!" And we were home.

Kathy and I got out and Gay transformed back into her humanoid shape, and I heaved a sigh. "Ladies, I don't know what comes next. Ashley told me that the combined inertia of other magic users would prevent anything bad from happening. But that didn't save Ashley, and maybe it can't save the Earth either. Any ideas?"

Kathy unlocked the door and we went in. Nobody said anything.

It started to get dark, and I napped a little, hoping it would help, knowing it probably wouldn't.

Something bumped on the window, and I nearly leapt out of my skin as I woke up. Gay was at the window, light saber drawn, and Kathy had her wand out. Kathy turned around, hearing my gasp as I awoke.

"Ah," she said. "Finished with your beauty sleep?"

I had to smile. "You tell me. So what did I miss?"

She turned back to the window. "There's a girl in the yard."

"What?"

She just waved at the window. It thumped again, so I got up and looked.

"Hell," I said. "That was a Shaun of the Dead reference, wasn't it?"

She nodded.

"So what's the news say?"

"Power's out."

I shot her a dirty look. "Gay?"

"Yeah, Boss?"

"What does the news say?"

They both jumped. "Hell, Boss," Kathy said. "I guess neither of us thought."

"Nothing about it on the news, Boss," Gay said. "Maybe it's just here?"

I shook my head. "Nah. I'll bet it started here, but they're zombies. They'll spread. Let's go out and look around. Gay, just chop off heads of any that get close, and we'll be fine."

Kathy grinned. "Cool!"

But it wasn't. Paris was a mess. It was full-on dark now, although the light from some fires helped mitigate the gloom. The moon was rising in the east, and I wondered when the Nazis would be coming.

Gay was having no difficulties at all defending us, so I didn't even bother with invisibility or a shield. The air was bracing, and I led my little band up towards the downtown.

"Oh, look," said Kathy. "The library's on fire!"

I snorted. "But the books are burning."

She shrugged. "Half the good ones have been phased out anyway. I don't mind the loss of the Twilight stuff. And I can Accio any book I like, now." She walked on, gleefully looking around at the carnage. "Hey, do you hear that?"

Gay looked up. "Sounds like jets."

It was, too. Bombers. I grabbed both Gay and Kathy and stepped over to the ruins of Jennette's house. It was two hundred miles away, but the flash still lit up the western sky.

"I guess I know why they didn't have anything on the news," I said.

"Huh," Kathy said. "I'm going to miss that town."

Another flash lit up the eastern sky behind us. We all whirled around. The moon was expanding, and it took me a moment to realize that half of it had turned into a cloud of rubble.

I cleared my throat. "Kathy?"

She nodded. "McDevitt, um, Moonfall, right?"

"I figure, yeah. I'm really thinking Ashley was wrong, Kathy. My myths are not survivable."

She looked at me, shocked. "What are you saying, Boss?"

"I'm saying that magic users should be raised on carefully selected myths. The ones I have in my head are adventurous, but unsafe. I'm the first new magic user in over a century, Kathy. A hundred years ago, the world people grew up in was already dangerous enough that they didn't have to invent stuff to scare themselves. They were scared enough with gods and demons, and their kids getting sick and dying."

I put arms around both of them. "As cool as you guys are, and as much as I love you, I don't think humanity can survive me."

Gay narrowed her eyes. "But you are also immortal. And I cannot violate my oath to protect you. So you're just going to have to think of a solution that includes your survival."

"Ditto to that, Boss," said Kathy. "Just ... fix the moon, OK?"

My head snapped around. "Oh!" I flipped my wand out and waved it at the moon. "Reparo!"

Nothing happened.

"Hell," I said.

"Light speed, Boss," said Kathy. "Wait a minute, then let's see."

Sure enough, a couple of seconds later, the rubble cloud did seem to be contracting instead of expanding, and I waited a few more seconds to be sure before clapping Kathy on the back. "Dude! It helped!"

"You want a, um, a power-up, Boss?"

I could feel the blush in the darkness. "Later, Cher. This will hold it for now. And besides, this took care of our Nazi problem at the same time, so let's let it sit a little bit first."

Pacing around the dragon skeleton, I tried to think. "The real problem here is that Ashley was the only other magic user I knew of. It seems to me that contacting others would have to help, right?"

They both murmured their agreement.

"But how does one contact a magic user if you don't know who or where they are?" I looked at Kathy.

"Owl?"

"Oh. Yes. And this is why I need minions. Acciotele-porting Owl. Acciopaper. Acciopen." The owl settled on Gay's arm, and I gestured for her to turn around so I could use her back as a writing surface.

"To any Magic User," I wrote. "Please contact me at your earliest opportunity; I need help." I looked at Kathy. "Who should I say it's from?"

She shrugged. "Violet?"

"Signed ... Violet. I hope that's not going to bite me in the ass." I folded the paper up and gave it to the owl. "Go, friend. Good luck."

It flapped up in the air and was abruptly gone. Thirty seconds later a portal opened up and a mechanical man clanked out.

Gay raised an eyebrow and nudged me in the ribs, and I had to suppress a laugh.

"Miss Vi-o-let." He spoke like Tik-Tok and I couldn't help but notice Kathy geeking out again on my other side. "My mis-tress begs the plea-sure of your com-pan-y at your ear-li-est con-ven-i-ence."

I chuckled. "Now would be fine. Lay on, MacDuff, and cursed be she who first cries, 'Enough!'" I stepped through the portal, my trusty companions at my side, and into ... London.

Not our London, mind you. This London, one could see, was not surrounded by traffic on the M25. There were no derivative bond traders here. This was not a mundane London.

It was foggy and there was a slight drizzle, but there was enough visibility to let me see some of it. Consider a steampunk London, you know, with difference engines and trains and the Royal Society and all that, then fast-forward it two hundred years. I can't even begin to describe it. There were bright lights, tube transport for people and goods zipping along above the streets, horse-drawn carriages with robot horses, and a looming light above that I could swear was a dirigible. The people were dressed in fantastic variety and were of all possible races, including one Thark that walked right in front of us as we tried valiantly to keep up with Tik-Tok.

Kathy boggled. "The sun doesn't set on this England, looks like, huh, Boss?"

Gay smiled. "Isn't this what England looks like?"

"No, Gay. Not in our world." I shook my head. "Can you fly up above this soup and see if their moon is OK?"

"Sure!" She shot up without even transforming, and was back in a couple of seconds, landing delicately on thrusters that folded into her hands as I watched. "No dice, Boss. It's still crunched."

"Damn. Thoughts, Kathy? Is this a timeline?"

"Gotta be, Boss. I've been to London, and it wasn't like this."

"Same moon, though?"

"There's just one Earth, right?"

"Maybe. Could be a Long Earth scenario or a scudder scenario or just about anything."

But Tik-Tok had led us into a building and opened the door to a quaintly decorated sitting room. There was a beautiful lady there in Victorian garb, and she looked up and smiled. "Ah, there you are. Thank you, Jeeves. Could you serve these ladies some tea?"

I curtseyed. I didn't even know I could. It just seemed the right thing to do.

She chuckled. "I am so very pleased to meet you, my dear. As you may have surmised, I am your direct predecessor in terms of age. I've often wondered what a modern magic user might be like."

I took a chair opposite her and sat. "Well. I'm not sure it was a good idea. I already got J ... uh, my progenitor killed."

"Oh, pish and tosh, dear. She'd been looking for a way out for centuries. You gave her the perfect excuse, if you'll pardon the indelicacy. I trust the old globe is tougher than you think."

"Have you looked at the moon lately?"

She blinked. "No, the weather is simply dreadful tonight. Why?"

"Gay? Can you project an image?"

"Sure, Boss." She held up a hand and it folded in a very complicated manner, extruding a lens.

The Victorian lady's eyes lit up. "Oh, how cunning!" Then she looked at what Gay was projecting and her skin, already quite pale, went bone white.

"What..." She swallowed. "What could possibly have done that?"

"A large mass traveling at a significant fraction of the speed of light, specifically targeting the moon."

"Speed of light?" She looked confused.

I put a hand over my eyes. "Einstein?"

"Never heard of the chap. Jew, is he? A Kabbalist, perhaps?" She was regaining her composure, it seemed.

"Physicist." I traded a look with Kathy. She widened her eyes a moment.

"The point is, ma'am," I continued, "that we've been forward in time a month, and the Earth is gone. And I don't know what to do about it. I had hoped you'd have some ideas."

She laughed. "The Earth? Gone? Child, far worse things than you have already come and gone in the millennia since the Earth coalesced from the void. Whatever you think you saw, it wasn't the Earth being gone. Not on this timeline, and probably not on any. Now let's not hear any more such defeatist nonsense, and have some nice tea. You'll see soon enough that events are never set in stone in the real world."

So we had some tea, and Gay flirted with Jeeves with only minimal success, and had a rather relaxing time until we heard the screaming in the street.

"Goodness," said the Lady. "Whatever could possibly be the matter?"

She hopped to her feet and wandered over to the door, opening it. The screaming became much louder, and we all went back out into the street, where people were in the process of being beamed up into what looked like an attacking fleet of flying saucers.

The Lady wrinkled her brow. "Preposterous! What could all this be?" Then she looked at me in alarm. "You! You've dreamed this up, haven't you!"

"Kathy?"

"I dunno, Boss, some kind of alien abduction trope, obviously."

I shook my head. "No, I remember this book, I just don't remember the author or anything about it. Yeah, it's definitely mine."

The Lady screeched, "Fix it! Fix it!" And then she was beamed up, too. And gone. The saucers flew away. Papers blew along the street, now empty and silent, although the lights were still bright and beautiful.

I wondered for how long. The mechanical men would surely keep things running for quite some time.

And that's when mummies banged into existence all around us and held all three of us tight before I could blink. The one holding me put a dusty-smelling hand over my mouth, presumably to block spells. I rolled my eyes and was just about to step away and clobber him when a voice rang out in the street.

"New mage! Do not flee!"

OK, I thought, let's see what this is about.

A small group of people were coming down the street towards us. As they resolved out of the fog, I could see there were four of them, all preternaturally beautiful young women, and I assumed therefore they must be magic users. One looked Oriental and was dressed in a kimono or robe of some kind, one was inky black and very tall, one looked round and brown and warm, and the fourth, the one who'd spoken, was topless, with a linen-y looking skirt, lots of gold, and beautiful almond eyes.

None of them seemed to like me much.

The leader, the one with the beautiful eyes, spoke again. "Mage, you have already killed two of our kind and have not even reached your full power. You have caused damage to the moon. We have done our best to scry your probable future and cannot.

"It is our conclusion that your progenitor was wrong to have brought you into our number, and that you are simply too dangerous to be permitted to continue as a magic user. We therefore invoke annullation."

"The hell you say," said Kathy, and teleported out of her mummy's grasp, wand in hand, and raised it to defend me and that's when the Oriental lady loosed a fireball towards me – the annullation spell? – and Kathy jumped in front of it and fell to the ground. With a vwoom next to me, Gay's light saber cut effortlessly through her own mummy and continued right behind me to free me, and I ran to Kathy's side.

Her invisible lower part was no longer there. She was bleeding at the interface – I realized all at once that the magic that kept her alive had been cancelled.

She smiled up at me and raised a hand, then knitted her brow. "Fly, fool." And she died.

Gay's arms enfolded me with steely strength and she leapt upwards with me, jets on, and just as we broke through the cloud deck into the clear air above and saw the dawn in the east, another fireball came up from the fog and winged her. A terrible metallic sound came from her leg. I twisted in her grasp, hugging her, and stepped back to Ashley's house again, and she let go and fell backwards.

"Shit, Boss," she said. "I can't transform. I think they broke me."

Kathy was dead. Again. I couldn't think.

"Boss? They can teleport, too. We have to keep moving, Boss." She struggled to her working foot.

With another bam! there were more mummies around us, and Gay swore.

"Dammit, Boss! You can't die!" She whipped out her light saber and cut all the mummies in half, then sheared off her dead leg, balancing perfectly on the other. Grabbing me in one hand, she jetted up into the sky.

Why couldn't I just die? Everybody else was.

"Boss," said Gay tenderly. "Come on. If they zap you back to human, you can't fix the Earth."

"I can't fix it anyway, Gay."

"Well, they sure can't. It's got to be a microblack hole down there, and it's already there. If you're baselined, we'll all die."

A dragon swooped at us, and without thinking I zapped it with an Avadra Kedavra. Kathy would have said something witty about an Unforgiveable Curse.

"I got it, Boss. I know how to fix it." And another fireball hit her then, right up her back. We started the long plummet back to Earth, right behind the massive corpse of the dragon, which was twisting in the wind just below us.

"Damn." Her voice had gone electronic. "OK, I still got it." Moving jerkily, she extruded a little unit – I realized it was the flux capacitor. She slapped it onto me, wrapped some duct tape around it (did she always have duct tape available?), hit it with some numbers, then threw me bodily away.

The last I saw of her, she was giving me a thumbs-up as I passed the 88 mph threshold and traveled through time.

Chapter 12

Coming Full Circle

IT WAS HOT, THEN COLD, THEN I FACE PLANTED IN A parking lot. I looked at the flux capacitor. It was a smoking ruin; I'd landed on it. I had no idea when or where I was.

Shakily, I stood up and Scourgified. It was early afternoon. Picking a direction at random, I walked off.

In just a few blocks, I saw I was back in Paris, miraculously restored. I had to laugh – I just kept ending up in this town.

Deciding to sit down for a nice coffee, I walked into a likely-looking little place, ordered a latte and a Danish, and sat down looking out at the sunshine. It was a lovely day today, with the powerfully blue sky that only Kansas can really give you, and I sighed as I bit into the pastry.

So did the kid leaning on a mop just behind me. Chuckling, I smiled at him – and froze.

Holy shit. His aura was blinding and I realized what Ashley had been talking about. I had really been a strong magic user even before she upgraded me.

Just then, the door tinkled again, and Ashley herself walked in. I watched helplessly as she sized the kid up, then walked over and ordered a large drink with ice.

What to do? What to do? Gay had obviously worked it out, but –

Ah.

Of course.

I took a deep breath, then blew it out. I squared my shoulders, swallowed, and stood up, then turned around and walked over to Ashley just as she was drawing her hand back with the drink. I took her by the wrist and looked into her eyes.

It was wonderful to see her again, and I couldn't help but smile. Her eyes flicked from me to the kid, then back, and then she gave me the drink, and nodded. She knew.

Carefully lining myself up, I drew my arm back. And doused my old self with an icy drink.

I was laughing so hard my sides were hurting – after all the unbelievable crap of the past few weeks, I thought I more than deserved it. I was having a fantastic time with myself! He had no idea who I was, of course. And I knew, oh, how very well I knew that he thought he wasn't keeping up his end of the conversation, but I saw what Ashley had seen in me that day, what had made her decide to throw caution to the winds and keep me around forever.

What I was going to do during the course of this day, of course, would undo that permanently. I wondered if I would slowly fade from existence as my magical future was snuffed out this evening. But I just couldn't bring myself to care. I was utterly and madly in love. Spellbound, you might say.

It wasn't the conversation. He was painfully shy, painfully quiet. But – forgive me for the woo-woo sound of it, because if you're not a magic user you'll never know – his true self, his being, radiated out like sunshine. I'd basked in his glow all day long; presumably this is what Kathy and Gay had felt as well.

And it was clear he felt it from me, too, as he hadn't from Ashley. We went for the same hike, and we were eating the same Chinese meal, but he was talking and laughing the whole time. We were just plain having a fantastic time, reveling in one another's existence and presence. This one day was worth a whole lifetime, a whole eternity, of lesser days.

And then it came round again, that same unbelievable fortune cookie text: "The distinctive and crucial feature in the study of man is the concept of action." I cracked up and laughed long and loud, finally just barely managing to squeak out, "... in bed!" before sailing off into further paroxysms, and he was laughing just as loudly. We were actually in the bed, or actually the futon in the front room because I couldn't help remembering Ashley's death as being associated with the bedroom, and so even while I was still laughing, I threw my arms around him and kissed him long and hard, and he responded in kind.

With my body right up against him like that, I could feel our energies resonate. It felt as though I could just pull him right into me, and it was gloriously like being in love. I melted closer, and only barely noticed the fact that our clothing was no longer in the way. Magic has a way of making easy things easier.

He had obviously had no problem this time around

knowing what to do, either. His massively erect manhood – how odd to imagine that it had once been mine – was crushed between us, and my entire interior seemed to have melted into a foggy warmth that simply demanded our complete sublimation into one another.

Abruptly he was inside me, moving slowly, and I couldn't possibly conceive of anything that could have been more right. I remembered my time with Kathy in this very futon, a couple of weeks from now, and how things had started breaking. This wasn't that. This was the opposite of that. Instead of my power being directed outwards, somehow it was being directed inwards, and instead of breaking, I could feel it building, and building, and I gazed into his eyes, which were my eyes, and he saw into mine, and we both went into the longest, sloppiest, most mind-blowing orgasm the world had ever known and just at the peak, he said...

"Oh, I see. You're me."

I nodded, and the power in both of us merged and the world exploded.

I knew no more.

Epilogue

I woke up alone, and yet not alone. There was no sign of my earlier self, and yet I could still sense his presence quite clearly, that same sunshine glow. I laid there a while until I realized I needed to pee.

It took me a while to realize it. It had been weeks since I had experienced it, after all. But yeah, definitely need to go to the bathroom.

Legs wobbly, I staggered into the bathroom, realizing that this would actually be the first time I'd gone to the bathroom as a woman.

The experience was prosaic. Afterwards, I looked blurrily into the mirror and realized I needed a shower. I sniffed. My breath stank. I was human.

And yet I felt his magic still. It was such a warming glow that I simply couldn't care less that I had bumped back down the evolutionary scale to H. sapiens. I was totally OK with it.

I took a shower for the first time in a month. It felt

really good. I managed to comb out my hair afterwards; it was surprisingly difficult to manage long hair, I found, and I thought maybe it might be a good idea to invest in a shorter haircut.

I'd need money.

I'd need a job.

Somehow it just didn't scare me any more. It was going to be just fine, I knew, without knowing how I knew.

Clean and radiant, I went into the front room and pulled on my clothing, found my wallet from my previous life, then went out and found some breakfast. Then I wandered aimlessly for a bit, and looked up to find that I'd somehow ended up outside the public library.

That did manage to penetrate the warm glow for a minute. I sighed. Then I went in and sat in that chair for a while.

The next thing I knew, a gentle hand was shaking me awake.

"Miss?"

I startled just a little too much, not too surprising given my recent life, and she jumped back as I rocketed to my feet, breathing hard.

"Oh, I'm sorry, dear." She furrowed her brow. "Are you all right? It's just that we're closing, and you've been dead to the world all day. Do you have anywhere to go?" She put a hand on my arm, very warmly.

I couldn't speak. I just couldn't.

Kathy wrinkled her brow. "Do I ... do I know you?"

I couldn't even breathe. I couldn't look away.

Her lips twitched, just a bit, and then she said... "Boss?"

I couldn't even beat my heart.

Kathy was transfixed, and the years were melting away from her as I watched. Her clothes got a lot looser, and her face got a lot scareder, and at the end of that, neither one of us could say anything.

I finally managed to take a breath. "Kathy?"

She nodded. "Yeah. Yeah."

I hugged her like she was back from the dead.

After we came out of our clench, she pulled back and said, "I remember everything. How ... how did you ... you've changed, Boss."

I nodded. "I'm human, Kathy. Which begs the question of just how you remember everything."

She stood up, clutching her skirt around her much-thinned waist, and went over to her desk and rummaged around in the drawer. With a smile, she held up a pencil.

"I'm not sure–" I started, but she'd already Accio'd new clothes before I could finish. I scratched my head. "Give me that pencil." She tossed it over as she bustled off to the restroom to change.

I caught it, waved it. "Accio money."

Nothing. Nothing at all. "Accio cookie." Zip. I picked up a piece of paper on the desk, tore the corner a little. "Reparo."

Nothing.

I was still standing there when Kathy came back, and I tossed her the pencil. "I don't get it. Ashley said your power was my power – but I've got no power and you're still magical."

She shrugged. "Then you've solved our problem.

Because your problem was that your power was killing us all."

"Nope. Gay solved it."

"So if I was here at the library, then logically ..."

"Gay's still in Ashley's garage, yeah."

She held out a hand. "Shall we?"

I took it, and we stepped to Ashley's house, which was still standing. I looked up at it. It seemed ... empty, somehow. I crunched over the gravel of the driveway to the front door and started to knock, then noticed the note taped to it.

"My dearest flower," it read, and that's as far as I got before it got blurry and I handed it to Kathy, who put a hand on my shoulder as she read it.

"My dearest flower – hey, Boss, looks like she remembers, too! So. My dearest flower, after some reflection I remembered everything of the timeline you've snipped off, oho, the plot thickens! and I felt what you did that evening to snip it. My feeling is that this path you have started down is promising, and it's clear that my active participation would only interfere. The house is yours, as I promised you last time around, and it is my dearest hope that your trusty companions will also be restored. Remember that I told you, although maybe not in so many words, that the Earth can abide even when you think all is lost. When you most need me, I will be there, but until then, I remain, at a distance, your loving Ashley."

She folded it carefully and tucked it into her pocket. "I'm going to keep this one for the scrapbook." She handed me a tissue, which I sorely needed at this point, and I blew my nose long and loud, making her laugh.

Then we went out to the garage, and pulled up the door to find the DeLorean. I looked at her, sitting there in the garage, slightly dusty, and wondered how this was supposed to work.

"You did it, Gay," I said, and put a hand on her hood. "You fixed the world."

Her engine started and her headlights came on.

"Oh!" said Kathy. "That's a good sign!"

With a sudden lurch, Gay transformed into her humanoid form. As always, it was a glory to behold, and I laughed in delight.

"Boss! Kathy!" she cried, and threw her arms around me, and I hugged her back fiercely while she held an arm out to Kathy as well.

Gay held me out at arm's length. "You've changed, Boss."

"I'm human, I guess. Maybe?"

She shook her head. "Nope, you're not, actually." She knelt down and looked at a point a couple of inches below my bellybutton. "But your daughter is."

"And so the Good Queen defeated the dragon, not with light sabers and fireballs but with love and understanding, and the dragon and the townspeople learned to live in harmony and lived happily ever after."

I ruffled her hair. "And now it's time for all the little princesses to go to sleep so they can grow up big and strong."

"Like Gay, Mommy?"

"Just like Gay, kiddo. Just like Gay."

"But I can't sleep, Mommy, I'm too excited!"

I smiled and kissed her. "Come on, poppet. You know we can't go tomorrow unless you get some sleep."

Jennie closed her eyes. I wasn't fooled for a minute, of course – she'd go to sleep when she was good and ready – but I crept softly out of her room and closed the door anyway, then wandered down to the kitchen to find Kathy.

"Cookies, Boss? I just finished 'em. Can't really have a picnic on the moon without cookies, after all."

"Thanks, Cher, don't mind if I do." I took one and sat gratefully. "That kid is running me ragged, Kathy."

"Pfft. Don't tell me you don't love it."

"I do love it. I love her. I think she's a keeper."

She just smiled.

It turned out, in case you were wondering, that my magic had indeed turned inwards. It was entirely focused on Jennie now, and presumably would be for some time. I could do magic at a subconscious level – but only if I perceived it to be in Jennie's best interest. I still couldn't do trivial magic at all, so Kathy had to Accio and Reparo things for me, but come on. I had a large house in the country, two boon companions who would demonstrably die to protect me and one of whom was also a car-slash-plane-slash-teleporting-time-machine, and an unlimited supply of money. I didn't really need trivial magic any more. I was already surrounded by it.

My days were full concocting a mythology that would reinforce human values and society, not tear it down, and I was field testing it all on Jennie while also trying to publish it out in the real world. Gay did wonderful illustrations for it. Bill said he knew some people who were going to really love it.

In the four years since Jennie's birth, I hadn't heard a peep from any other magic user. They were out there, all right. They might even have been aware of the timeline that almost was. But if so, they seemed to agree that things had been diverted onto a safe track.

And so the Good Queen defeated the Earth-devouring black hole, not with whiz-bang magic and gadgetry but with the gallant help of her two friends, and the Queen and the little princess and their companions lived happily ever after.